QUEER VOICES

QUEER VOICES

Poetry, Prose, and Pride

EDITED BY
Andrea Jenkins,
John Medeiros, and
Lisa Marie Brimmer

MINNESOTA
HISTORICAL
SOCIETY PRESS

mnhspress.org

The Minnesota Historical Society Press is a member of the Association of University Presses.

Manufactured in the United States of America

10 9 8 7 6 5 4 3 2 1

♾ The paper used in this publication meets the minimum requirements of the American National Standard for Information Sciences—Permanence for Printed Library Materials, ANSI Z39.48-1984.

International Standard Book Number
ISBN: 978-1-68134-122-4 (paper)
ISBN: 978-1-68134-140-8 (e-book)

Library of Congress Cataloging-in-Publication Data available upon request.

This and other Minnesota Historical Society Press books are available from popular e-book vendors.

CONTENTS

INTRODUCTION

Andrea Jenkins, John Medeiros, and Lisa Marie Brimmer, editors

Welcome, reader, to the culmination of years of planning and extremely hard work by the finest and best queer literary talent the Twin Cities have to offer! This collection of queer voices features both emerging and established writers of the LGBTQIA+ community who have read with one of Minnesota's proudest and longest-running literary programs: the Queer Voices Reading Series.

This book, like the series, houses the annals of queer writers and their unique stories. It provides readers with a wealth of prose, poetry, and pride. It also puts a spotlight on a reading series that has become not only one of Minnesota's most important literary institutions but also a national model.

To appreciate how this book came to fruition, it helps to understand a brief history of the Queer Voices Reading Series and the community that has supported it over the years.

The Making of a Community

The Queer Voices Reading Series, curated by John Medeiros and Andrea Jenkins since 2005, began as the LGBT Reading Series of SASE: The Write Place, an organization founded by writer Carolyn Holbrook. Says Carolyn: "We operated out of a small office in the arts-centric building in South Minneapolis, but we conducted our programs out in the community, with a particular focus on underrepresented cultural and racial minorities. We worked with writers in all genres, from fiction to memoir to documentation. SASE was founded with a deeply held belief that the world is a large writing tablet, and that the act of putting pen to paper is one of the most powerful tools we have to create an environment of civic literacy in which everyone's voice is heard."

Two of SASE's programs focused specifically on LGBTQIA+ communities. One program focused on short-term residencies for gay, lesbian, bisexual, and transgender youth. The second was started in 2001 as part of the About Town Reading Series, a program that gave writers an opportunity to curate monthly readings in community gathering places of their own choice. In 2005, when John Medeiros and Andrea Jenkins—both prominent and published writers themselves—took over the helm of Queer Voices About Town, the series' momentum grew, and it soon became one of the strongest programs within SASE. The program grew even stronger the next year when SASE merged with Intermedia Arts, a community-focused arts center that uses art as a catalyst for social change. In 2016, Lisa Marie Brimmer— equity and public programming manager with Intermedia Arts— joined John and Andrea to recruit even more diverse voices to be part of our larger LGBTQIA+ literary community.

The Queer Voices Reading Series thrived over the years not only because it provided queer writers a safe place to share our thoughts and our writings, but because, in doing so, it also created a community that believes in the power of the word. A community that believes in fostering its strength and its unity through literature. A community that believes in achieving social change through its words.

The Making of an Anthology

The same spirit of community that was created by the Queer Voices Reading Series is responsible for the anthology you hold in your hands. Like the series, this book now assumes a vital place in the new literary canon.

Queer Voices: Poetry, Prose, and Pride is the by-product of a united community. The lush complexity of voices—from the cries of gay men who have lost lovers and themselves to disease and war, to the shouts of lesbians as they meet their queer idols and still fight for basic human rights, to the whispers and defiant declarations of transgender men and women who find themselves navigating a new world, to the myriad reflections of the bisexual and the gender fluid—these are the voices that make up our community. These are the new and emerging voices that still need to be heard, both in person and in print.

The voices featured in this anthology write to further understand this world and who we are in it. We write to embrace that understanding and to share it with others. This has been one of the most successful evolutions of the Queer Voices Reading Series, and one we hope will further evolve with the publication of this book.

Moving Forward

We regret that since the production of this book began, Intermedia Arts closed its doors permanently, leaving a hole in the Twin Cities arts scene—and in the Queer Voices fabric. And while we are hopeful that the series will find a new home in the near future, we will miss Intermedia Arts and its staff who were so committed to its mission to use art as a catalyst for social change. And so we dedicate this anthology to the legacy of Intermedia Arts. May it pay homage to the myriad voices that have shaped it over the past twenty years, and may it pave the way for new voices yet to be heard.

QUEER VOICES

ELIZABETH JARRETT ANDREW

Elizabeth Jarrett Andrew is the author of *Hannah, Delivered, Swinging on the Garden Gate, On the Threshold: Home, Hardwood, and Holiness,* and two books on writing: *Living Revision: A Writer's Craft as Spiritual Practice* and *Writing the Sacred Journey: The Art and Practice of Spiritual Memoir.*

Wearing Bifocals

I recently passed that marker of middle age and got bifocals. Actually, they're "progressive lenses," so they draw no distinct line between the prescription for what's close and what's distant. For three weeks I felt dizzy. I had trouble climbing stairs. Reading in bed gave me a headache. But then my eyes *learned*; they transitioned seamlessly and saw the whole.

I find this stunning. We humans have the inherent capacity to move between two seemingly diametrically opposed ways of seeing, near or far, either/or, and make of them both/and. I'd lost this ability, I'd regained it with new glasses, and only now can I appreciate the miracle.

Too bad that the learning curve back to nondualistic seeing is so damn painful.

For instance: the moment I smashed through my presumed heterosexual identity. The year was 1992. I was twenty-two, standing just inside the door of my first apartment, and suddenly the glass box of others' assumptions, which I'd unknowingly taken on as my own, shattered. I stood there sobbing, gasping for breath. To move anywhere meant stepping on shards.

I wept for all the years I'd misunderstood myself, cramming the breadth of my experience into a small and cramped story. I wept because the name that best described me was associated with many things I was not—promiscuous, wishy-washy, someone who might don a dildo to march in the Pride parade. I wept for the very ugliness and inaccuracy of the word, the initial "bi" hacking at "sex" with its unnecessary overemphasis, the "ual" pointing an accusatory finger. I wept because I knew society, and my parents especially, would not like this new identity.

With the hindsight of twenty-five years, I now know I wept that day in my lonely, sun-streaked apartment because I'd broken out of one box to step into another, admittedly more accurate and free, but still a box.

A friend of mine died recently. Jeanne Audrey Powers was one of the first women ordained in the United Methodist Church. She worked for the General Conference in Manhattan and traveled the globe, hobnobbing with top religious leaders of every stripe. Just before she retired, she came out as lesbian at an international conference, sending waves of dismay—and change—throughout the global church. She kept an apartment in Minneapolis and attended my small neighborhood church, which was how I came to work for a brief spell as her personal secretary.

Working for Jeanne Audrey meant handling mundane tasks like sorting mail, paying bills, and balancing her checkbook. This giant of a woman was paralyzed by a stack of unopened mail. I'll always remember one evening when I helped her host a women's gathering at her high-rise apartment. I carried a bag of fruit and vegetables into her kitchen, pulled a built-in cutting board out from under the counter, and began chopping. Jeanne Audrey entered—and nearly fell over. "What's that?" she asked of the cutting board. Jeanne Audrey had lived twenty years in her apartment and had never once sliced a carrot there.

Jeanne Audrey, unlike me, thrived on conflict. Once, when she joined a board for a church organization and was asked to submit a photo, she sent an image of herself topless, displaying a gorgeous tattoo descending over her mastectomy scar. I remember her at the Re-Imagining conferences in the mid-nineties, the gatherings at which feminism collided with the mainline church denominations; Jeanne Audrey sniffed out the conservative infiltrators and press reps, brought them coffee, and engaged them in lengthy, honest, and disconcertingly intimate conversations. By the end of the day they were exchanging phone numbers. Jeanne Audrey was formidable in her ability to transform enemies into friends.

In my hand I hold the blue sheet of paper announcing her death and ponder what made this inept woman so effective at building connections across difference. She was a feminist, she was a woman attracted to women, but I suspect the secret to Jeanne Audrey's reconciliatory powers was that she loved these boxes not for her identity but for their contents. I write this in her honor.

• • •

I was unbelievably blessed in my coming out. My parents were warm and open-minded. The church of my childhood preached and lived a loving God. In my early twenties I intuited that my life force would not loosen or move until I turned clear eyes toward my sexual desires, so I found a spiritual director willing to explore sexuality as a gateway into relationship with divinity and joined a small church that proclaimed a deliberate welcome to gays and lesbians. When bisexuality and transgender concerns percolated into the public consciousness in the early nineties, the congregation hosted adult education sessions to explore broadening its welcome. I was in the chapel listening to a panel of bi visitors when I first understood what bisexuality meant. My church taught me.

The one glitch in my coming out was that I had no partner. For many queer people, the gender of a romantic partner finally exposes the deceptions we've perpetuated and foists us out of the closet. I had dated a guy for three years in college—that was it. No experiments with girls, no one-night stands, just the bare ache of my body. My attraction to others was alive, diverse, and unexpected. I felt like a fraud because I had no tangible proof.

For me coming out was not about claiming a sexual reality. The word *bisexual* felt all wrong, limiting identity to sexuality alone when in fact my body, mind, and spirit were all formed of this multifarious love. The name seemed to divide the world into a dichotomy of gender utterly contrary to my own fluid and flexible experience. Only recently did I learn that the "bi" actually refers to heterosexuality and homosexuality, and glad as I am for this, the prefix still makes me wince. I use it less and less, not because it's easier to pass now that I'm in a committed relationship—with a woman, mind; I mean pass as lesbian, another word that feels like broken glass—but because it's so inadequate. My partner, who is eight years younger, uses the term *queer*, which has grown on me over time; it's elusive and strange and inclusive of gender-bending as well as sexual attraction. Queer inhabits the outskirts. I like queer's perch and perspective. If I'm queer, you can't nail me down. I'm also more hip. If I'm bisexual, you can carbon-date me as coming out in the nineties.

But queer also perpetuates a polarity—straight and queer—that's inaccurate. Bisexuals can imagine and inhabit both of these worlds. All this packaging limits a self which I'm discovering to be a fathomless source of surprise.

But at first, coming out helped me name an essential quality of my being. I needed the box so I (and others) could see its contents.

Okay, I still need it. Take today: I'm hawking my novel about a home-birth midwife at the Twin Cities Birth and Baby Expo, with booths for the latest cloth diaper designs on my left and a maternity yoga center on my right. An endless stream of glowing pregnant women push strollers past my table. I'm seated at the very hetero heart of our culture, and my queer identity is, once again and against my will, buried. These strangers can easily assume their reality is mine. After all, my readers assume I'm straight, that I've given birth, that I'm a midwife. Over and over, I say, "It's *fiction*."

I almost wish my booth were topped with a sign saying "Bisexual!" with an arrow pointing at me. I need the name, the box, maybe even the dildo, to break through others' quick and flimsy constructions. Out here it's not enough to hold my contradictions privately, because then they're ignored or denied or, worse, persecuted. I need to claim bisexual, if not for my own sake, for the sake of complicating our collective stories.

Actually, I encountered two glitches in coming out. I'd planned to tell my parents on a summer visit to New York. I'd bought plane tickets. But just weeks before my flight, we learned that my sister was pregnant, out of wedlock, with a man my parents and I both despised and mistrusted. My mother and father were devastated. They wept, they were furious, they felt their world crumble. When I finally sat them down and announced I was bisexual, my mother's face blanched and fell, and then she said, "Thank God you're not pregnant."

• • •

Unless you're outrageous and gregarious in your sexual exploits, bisexuality is mostly below the surface—a vibrant, continual embrace of contradictions; an aesthetic; a saturation of the self. While everyone around you (trans friends gratefully excepted) seems satisfied to fit into dualistic structures of gender and sexuality, you find yourself muttering, "But—but—" Bisexuality is nonduality made flesh. It's a spiritual gift.

Of course all sexuality is a spiritual gift. It's just that socially normative sexuality bears socially normative spiritual gifts. And our culture manages to deny even these.

Gifts on the margins, then, are especially invisible. Even to those who embody them. On a recent book tour of two-year colleges in rural Wisconsin, hotbed of conservative Christianity, I was asked several times by various students with shaved hair or pierced eyebrows and voices edgy with hurt, "Is it possible to be both queer and spiritual?"

Is it possible to be both/and? Listen to your bodies.

For the ten years of writing that novel, I swam in the amniotic fluids of birthland, where women's bodies demonstrate an animal wisdom we in our most sophisticated, technological institutions can't begin to comprehend; where our culture fears bodies, especially women's bodies; where pain is a veil women pass through to meet new life. What does birth—natural birth, traditional birth—reveal about our essential humanity? And when our beginnings are meddled with, by medicine, fear, economics, convenience, how are our spirits affected? For a decade I romped in the subversive world of midwives and loved it—as a novelist. It wasn't mine, but it became mine. In the limitless liberty of fiction, my external reality—that I was a bisexual woman in a same-sex partnership and with an adopted daughter—mattered not a whit.

Except it did. My questions were an evolution of questions I'd been asking all along. What does it mean to be embodied spirit—in *this* body, with its unexpected attractions? We are our bodies, and we are not our bodies, and how can this be? What happens at that moment when breath enters flesh and the whole magnificent journey of being spirit incarnate begins? What happens when it ends?

Turns out bisexuality colors everything: my favorite movie stars, my companion in bed, how I've pieced together work, the God I worship. Certainly my experience of gender. Certainly my lifelong obsession with that ultimate of paradoxes: We are magnificent, mysterious energy inhabiting, for a short but beloved spell, matter. And the form of that matter is magnificently varied.

Which reminds me of another moment from my coming out story. On the Sunday I had determined to come out at church—during Joys and Concerns, when the community shares its prayers—Jeanne Audrey had just healed from her mastectomy. We both raised our hands for the mic. I shook with nerves about calling myself bisexual in front of God and these people, so I was relieved when the usher handed the mic first to Jeanne Audrey. She stood, affectionately stroked her chest, and thanked God for her new body, which was clearly missing a breast.

Moments before I came out in church, Jeanne Audrey as a form of prayer publicly fondled herself. It was as though the universe had conspired to say to me, "See? Your inner contradictions are nothing compared with what's possible."

I wish in response to those young, searching Wisconsin students I'd mentioned the Native tradition of honoring Two Spirits, those who manifest all genders or are attracted to all genders, as spiritual leaders. Who better than queer folk to navigate the dynamic intersection between matter and energy? By virtue of our bodies, we're much accustomed to traversing multiple worlds. And in one of the more difficult spiritual realities to comprehend, the further a person is pushed by difference or discrimination to the edges of society, the deeper the well of grace made available to them. If only their hearts are open to it.

As a Christian I mischievously consider Jesus a great Two Spirit, both gentle and fierce, tender to John and sweet on Mary, one foot in our gritty unjust world and the other in a numinous Present. I say this playfully but I'm serious. If you're looking for a model of nonduality, of embodying and transcending oppositions, it's hard to find better than Jesus. *In Christ there is neither Jew nor Gentile, neither slave nor free, nor is there male and female, for you are all one.*

But here's the trouble: There's no better model for dualism (black-

and-white thinking, good-and-bad judgment, the in-crowd and the out) than the church.

I prefer to hunker down in Christianity's foundational, defining message of incarnation. Daily I consider Teresa of Avila's warning: "Christ has no body now on earth but yours, no hands but yours, no feet but yours." So divinity is in this bisexual libido and this body that rebels against cosmetics (the evening of my high school prom, my mother chased me around the house insisting, "You *will* wear blush!"), and in these breasts I pumped every two hours for an entire month before a generous woman gave birth to Gwyn, my daughter, so I could nourish her with my milk; divinity is in my heart stilled by prayer and in my frantic churning mind; divinity is in my abundant leg hair which Gwyn tries to braid, calling me "Mr. Mom." God has no sense of smell but yours, no capacity to touch but yours, no evolution but yours . . . I train my bi eyes on all this wretched glory and try to see it.

• • •

I need—we all need—progressive lenses. We need to imitate my parents, who recognized my sister's terrible mistake and chose to love her and her son regardless—who turned to me after I came out and said, "We don't understand this, it might take us a while, but know that we love you." We need to imitate a woman giving birth, holding tightly to her hopes and plans and then releasing them in favor of the mysterious workings of her body. We need to imitate Jeanne Audrey, who at eighty-five was afflicted with aphasia and blindness; she had no living relatives and was steadily losing her ability to read, write, speak, and think. Her letter arrived yesterday. "I have had such a full and meaningful life," she wrote. "It's important that you understand that this was not a 'suicide' as commonly understood, but it was very much a death with dignity." I hold the page in my hands. Her spirit is alive and kicking there, ardent, strong, and I laugh out loud because with her final act Jeanne Audrey managed to befriend even death.

We're such beloved bundles of contradictions! I am shaman and shithead; Jesus is God and man; the earth is passive and subtly dynamic; we are all both male and female, absolutely marginalized and fundamentally centered, broken and perfect, unborn and born and always coming alive. There's a Hasidic tale I love about a Jew who walked through life carrying two verses from the Torah on slips of paper, one in each jacket pocket. He referred to one and then the other throughout the day. In his left pocket the verse read, "Dust to dust." In his right pocket the verse read, "For you the universe was made." The paradox is acute and resplendent. "I am Nobody—who are you?" asks Emily Dickinson; "I am large; I contain multitudes," exudes Walt Whitman. Both are true. The slips of paper feel heavy in my pockets. I can read only one at a time.

But read them I can! Every morning, this bisexual woman dons bifocals and rises to the work of seeing, really seeing, this sparkling, complicated world.

Cole Bauer grew up in northwest North Dakota and later moved to Minneapolis, where he earned a BA in studies in cinema & media culture and German studies from the University of Minnesota in 2010. He spends much of his free time watching films and birding.

Lipstick Elephants

And so I told her of the tan man, a timeless
New Mexican transformed by desert testing
of speed cars and cloud seeding
and of Michael the drubbed, constantly
a proclaimer of self-defiance who, like a
battering ram
took his beatings on the rocky outcrop
of the steps to his apartment

She laughed, this is nothing
and so I gave her keywords:
tackle boxes, citrus cleaner, Ray-Bans,
beds in Berlin, and by beds, I mean
more than one, days-old sweat
and mystery meat only a German
would swallow

She took a sip of some sweet tea
and denied my advancements
on leaving this conversation
tell me of the last love—
Viktor, the Franklin Bank clerk
and of Ukrainian smooth skin,
with bluebonnet eyes that hid a history
of shipment from Kiev's most
"important" regional hospital system
He scratched along in languages
incomplete enough to understand

liquored slurs of hayseed
whose value could have been called
lump sum
Ignoring the fascinating wildlife
    of southern meat market offerings with
our tastes for one another
we parted our ways amidst a fling
that shattered the way hayseeds do
business with folks like us
His blues hid it all from me
and I could only nod

She told me
tell of him, the first one, so many
years ago
and so I began
with my first crush, a boy for which I fawned
and jerked my little knob at the back of the bus
hoping, in all secrecy, that he would turn and see
then came the day, out behind his uncle's old barn
we swiped some schnapps and cracked sticks,
cracked knuckles, and under my motionless guidance
he drew near and I put my lips on his, slowly,
and began to run my tongue along his
teeth
Soon I tasted uncured varnish on the floorboards
of an attic room he called his, and I let it happen
a force of Southern hospitality with smooth
molasses motions that even Jimmy Carter
would pray his
What does a boy do? Like him
when the truth reveals itself in such a way
like that?

I let the linen curtains curtail round my body
and dreamt of circus elephants with lipstick
and rubber wristbands that say

welcome to the greatest show on Earth!
can I make your wildest dreams come true?

There were many others, a storyboard of
haves and have-nots, sparklers, beachcombers,
tax collectors and one or two who helped me discover
that waterboarding can have its sexual advantages
various shiftings of love or whatnot
each to end with sifting sand as its base
relations bubbling up, past and present, to
a world that remains apathetic at best
You can say goodnight moon, goodnight stars,
but the residual energies of high-tide beach running
can only remind one of how close
sadness is to the surface—

She sat quietly, me now a friend unbeknownst
waiting for me as a prism in the night for
some stray light to give her
illumination
and to know where I stand, amongst
a forest of wild animals
putting lipstick on elephants
I can only recall
so many
they've come and gone
out like last week's leftovers
and so I go too, cutting my beard
making morning prayers out of habit
slipping on my sunglasses
I open the door to exhaustive
heat, knowing full well that
I will wipe my brow more
than once today

Rochester

Let's go dancing in Rochester tonight
I'll bring my aviators and you,
bring the stack of wonder comics
to ensure proper escape from this town!
The sun will warm our chilled cheeks
and our smiles will grow as we see
ahead of us, a night of joy
The car plugs along, down the road, please
pass me the egg salad sandwich and
open the windows
I'll puff this last cigarette and you do
up your hair in the mirror
And we'll look cool and hold hands
walking toward the world-famous
Rochester Rocket Dance Club
where Yuri once laid eyes on a beautiful
woman only to be denied because he
couldn't say the words,
"Follow me, and I shall show you."
As a tomcat sits outside the door and
red paint has splattered on the windowsill
someone whispers *r o c k e t f u e l*
When we open the door, don't forget
my nails are painted and your eyes
talk loud—they will ask us to dance
Can you handle that?
Because I can, if only you
smile and nod in my direction
when Yuri's song comes on
ghost or not, myth or not, love or not
we know the truth as our delight
at least for tonight, in Rochester town

RYAN BERG

Ryan Berg's debut book, *No House to Call My Home: Love, Family, and Other Transgressions,* won the 2016 Minnesota Book Award for General Nonfiction and the 2016 Media for a Just Society Award and was listed as a Top Ten LGBTQ Book of 2016 by the American Library Association. Ryan has been awarded residencies from The MacDowell Colony and Yaddo.

Drown

Everything is coming in waves today. You can't remember the last time you felt like this. For months now you've been buried under a glacial sheet, all light faded. Only momentary glimmers burn through where you warm up and feel anything at all.

But now a thawing has begun.

You heard about him on the news. At first he seemed to be just another casualty, sacrificed to the city. When they started talking about him trapped under the ice, frozen and unreachable, you began to take notice, finding yourself turning on the TV only to hear about him. After the sixth day he was discovered, they said his name was Miguel Flores. Before that he was only known as "the body." For six days, nameless. The TV anchorwoman said that he wandered out onto the frozen lake in Prospect Park ignoring all the signs posted warning him not to. The ice cracked; he fell in. Witnesses said after he managed to pull himself out, he started to walk away, but the ground beneath him weakened again and split. He sank back into the water. Authorities had no leads as to his identity. Seems that no one was looking for him; no one knew he was missing from their lives.

Before you saw him on TV you hadn't left the apartment in three days. The only time you found the strength to get out of bed was to pour another drink. But since hearing his story, you sit in front of the television waiting to find out what's happened. There's a small stirring of life inside you again. That ice, interrupted. The anchorwoman says, "They can't locate the body" or "waiting for the body to surface," and you know he's alone, pressed up against the cold skin of the lake, looking through it, watching the milky and fluid faces of onlookers, the wave and ripple of winter elm branches, the world, just over there, just on the other side, unreachable. The cold in his body is all fire and his fingers scratch and scratch the surface that separates here from there. He's become leaden and breathless and the aperture of soft light floating above him dims and fades as you imagine his body sinking further into the bitter murk.

● ● ●

Cards on the table, mud in the doorway. Miguel picked up his satchel and took one more swallow of milk before opening the front door. Typically he woke before anyone else in the shelter, the room still dark and seeming foreign. Although he'd lived there for two months he still woke most mornings confused, disoriented. Then slowly the dark and cold would become familiar as he'd lie in his bed, blinking his eyes, trying to focus on things around him. In the dark everything always looked different. In the muted light the old man sleeping next to him they called Dollar had the skin of Miguel's mother. Soft, almost transparent. Lying there on his side he'd watch her sleeping in the bed next to him, her snores a shrill thunder. Pete, two beds down, looked like Ms. Connie, one of the day counselors at the shelter, when he slept. In the darkness Pete's thin nose and high cheekbones mashed into the thick and flat bulldog grimace Ms. Connie made as she cooked in her feverish rage. Miguel knew these transformations were only the dark playing tricks on his eyes, but still, secretly, he liked to think that while sleeping, people became who they couldn't be in the light.

He stepped outside, swinging his satchel over his shoulder. He stuck his bare hands in his coat pockets, shielding them from the cold. The trees lining the wide expanse of Eastern Parkway were frozen in lifeless postures—all naked without their leaves—and the snow underfoot crunched as Miguel walked down the sidewalk. Some things he couldn't get used to no matter how ordinary they were to life here. The sound of snow grinding under his weight: he wished his mother could hear it. It was a pure sound. It sounded exactly the way snow should sound. In his letter to her today he would try to describe it.

Dawn was just breaking in the east, casting an orange glow over the snow-covered streets. The light split and burst into glimmers. He made the sign of the cross as he always did when he saw something he considered a miracle. Last month was the first time Miguel ever saw snow and he was amazed how the white could blanket even this chaotic city into quiet. A bitter gust of wind shot up behind him as he crossed into the park. He shoved his hands deeper into his pockets and moved his fingers around. The joints were becoming sore from the cold.

Miguel spent most mornings in the park no matter the weather. He liked the idea of this pocket of nature immune to the flux and buzz of city life. He'd sit on a bench deep within the park and watch people with their dogs, trying to imagine what kind of life they lived. New York seemed full of possibility and he planned to take advantage of that. Once he got a job, found a permanent place to live, he'd be able to send money back home to Honduras and show his mother that he'd succeeded.

A tall woman led by a small, tottering dog walked up along the pathway. The dog stopped at Miguel's feet and sniffed. He reached down and let the dog nuzzle its wet snout into his palm. He looked up and smiled at the woman. To his surprise the woman smiled back. Sometimes his attempts here at greeting strangers were completely ignored.

"Good morning," Miguel said in his broken English.

The tall woman smiled and nodded, her red knit cap falling forward a bit. She pulled it down with her free hand, then tugged at the dog's leash. They made their way down the snow-covered path toward the lake. Miguel's plan for the day was to write his letter to his mother and then begin his job search. Before he left his cousin's house in South Carolina two months ago he'd heard that there was construction work in New York. The city had always intrigued him. He'd heard stories from relatives and friends back in his town in Honduras about the throngs of people filling the streets, the enormous buildings that glowed at night. He decided to see it for himself.

The woman with the red cap walked down the sloping path with her dog until they disappeared completely. Miguel suddenly got up and started walking. He kept a safe distance, didn't want her to think he was following her. But maybe he was in some way. Her smile was so gentle that it drew Miguel in. He didn't want to let go of that kindness.

The hardest thing for him about living in New York wasn't the cold or not having any money. It was the lack of connection, the feeling that he somehow didn't belong. Miguel was astonished when people would bump into him on the street and keep moving as if he didn't even exist. The woman with the red cap showed him he wasn't completely invisible here. Someone could see him.

The path emptied into a small clearing that centered on a lake. A boathouse sat on the other side. The woman was already making her way up the next hill that led toward the opposite side of the park. Her little dog panted as it scrambled along next to her, its breath making a steam engine trail.

Miguel stopped and stared out at the frozen lake. Everything here was so still and quiet. The surface had grown a rigid and solid crust of ice that seemed impenetrable. He carefully made his way down to the edge of the lake and tapped his foot against the surface. It felt like concrete. He stepped out with both feet now firmly set on the ice and jumped a little, testing the durability. He landed solid, the surface unmarked.

Miguel had forgotten about the woman with the red cap who was now nearing the top of the hill and would soon disappear onto the other side. The expanse of ice had completely captured his attention. Miguel stepped out further onto the lake, his arms outstretched as if balancing on a beam. He bounced up and down every few steps to ensure the floor's stability, making his way toward the center.

He wished he had a camera. This would be a great picture to send to his mother. Miguel walking on water.

His smile distorted when his footing gave way and the ice beneath him cracked and crumbled. The shock of the water took his breath away as he plunged under the dark surface. He couldn't tell if he was floating up or sinking down until his head bumped against the ice. Frantically, he pressed up, feeling around until he found the hole he crashed through. When his head broke the surface he gasped, his lungs burning with cold. Miguel blinked and blinked but all he could see was white.

He screamed for help, his voice ripping through the quiet morning. He clawed, digging his nails into the ice, but there was nothing to hold onto. He hoisted himself up onto his elbows and tried to swing his legs out but they felt like fallen logs. He had to look down to make sure his knee was propped against the solid face of the lake. He slowly pressed and leaned forward until he crawled out completely. His body felt scalded as the wind picked up, brushed against the dry tree branches. Miguel pushed himself up to his feet, fought for his balance, and began to walk toward solid ground.

Through his burning vision he saw a woman running toward him down the hill. For a moment he thought it was his mother but then the red cap came into focus. She was screaming at him to lie down, spread his body weight out, but he couldn't hear her. Not that he would have understood anyway.

Miguel took another step and the ice under him again cracked apart, this time the hole too big and his body too exhausted to fight. He sank and surrendered to the slow, pulling current.

• • •

The TV light flickers against your wet cheeks. Finally the divers found him, bloated and stiff, the pallor of lilacs. He had a name, Miguel Flores. He was a twenty-three-year-old immigrant from Honduras who arrived in New York only two months ago. You watch the anchorwoman talk about this man who silently slipped away, no one noticing he was gone.

Stephani Maari Booker of Minneapolis writes works for the page and for performance in which she wrestles with her multiple marginalized identities: Black, lesbian, lower-class, nerdy, and sexy. She has poetry, nonfiction, science fiction, and erotic fiction in many publications. For more information about Stephani's work, go to https://www.goodreads .com/athenapm.

Mango

Sunshine sweet thing,
Let your sugar rain
all over me
as I lie back
and taste your golden meat
with my skin.

Sweet sticky thing,
as the Players used to swing.
Juicy fruit, like Mtume,
you make me want to sing.

Shine your juicy fruitiness
all over me.
Rain your sweet stickiness
all over me.

A sweet sticky mess
clean as sun and rain.
No muddy marks of chocolate,
no tacky crusts of honey,
no shocking ice cream,
no fleeting whipped cream.
Nothing for me
but my sweet sticky thing.

My sunny sweet sticky thing.
My sugar rain.
My juicy, fruity thing.
Make me shine
all over.

Wavelengths

Hearing
the frequency,
soft cycling
of inhale
and exhale

Watching
the undulations,
crests and troughs,
of breaths
on a breast

Reaching
to caress
the amplitude
from sternum
to areola

Touching
the wavelengths
of respiring,
radiating
life.

LISA MARIE BRIMMER

Lisa Marie Brimmer is a queer, black, transracial adoptee writer and cultural strategist. They hold an MA in English literature from the University of St. Thomas. Lisa's work engages with environment, kinship, and culture while plotting intersectional black queer liberation. More information about Lisa and her writing can be found at: lisamariebrimmer.com & @2speakease.

i go on

a kiss / so sultry subversive / special
some thick synergy / stewed perpetual war / left on
the lip of a glass / so many guns / on your lips
a *scratch of red bleeding*
the cue ball / in the pocket where / your hands
in my pocket where / you pushed me / on the pool table
hot lightning / hot heat / kiss, then green, then wet
then hung / a thing wrung out / the cheap grating

of mouth on / perpetual mouth / devotion / a netted
enclosure / a kiss hides a thing / maybe a resolution
an adjustment / a thing amended / to form confusion
my lips are pursed / my teeth / are sucked / a violent
imagination / a clavicle unlocked / a hip bone unhinged

i got one phone call / and my damp hand / it was easy
falling in love / with you / while the world was on fire
and the matchbook got rained on / and the wine went
missing / and a car wouldn't start / and upstairs
a baby can't sleep / so none of us can sleep / a cliché
at best / an immediate building up / a scar time / i go on

and what i mean is / it could solve the misery
for a minute / or what i mean is / it could solve the misery for two
we build life up to be / a great thing / a leaping
out of windows / in tandem / calling ourselves
firecrackers / looking for pride / and whether

it's a boyish mood / or a boi-ish affectual mood
or simple boi-ish affection / the very unprecedented
generosity your skin / offers is a much-needed / respite
from the friction / or the anticipated friction / of the cut
mango eye / i go on sucking the mango / the eye i cut /
the dressing / the i sucking / my teeth / the meat from
the thick-skinned mango / the glean of the unused knife
i go on / eating the seed dry

i go on / resisting the shrivel
the quiet / the closet / the dry pout
the northwesterly / the newscast
orlando / philando / chicago / the car alarm
we don't even hear / the radio / anymore

the slow blown heels / the thing
which is darkness / the not darkness

and i go on / i think sometimes / we are darkness
is not / the same / as drowning
the drop-off / the break / the breaking / the
broken / the dense brown / mouth of smoke / i go on

believing / to grope the eager / the slender hip / so many guns
on your hips / on your jaw / the groan-creak
you scare the dog / straight / out the back door
to piss / and act / as if he never
learned / how to
be good / good boy / how to
heel / who's a good boy / how to
hump the dress / pillows in the front / instead of
your thigh / the good boy / the cut i / the cut mango
the scratch of red bleeding / your perfect mouth
your goodbye / the back of your dark neck

some dogs don't learn / they can't jump
on everyone's lap / some dogs never learn
some dogs make church / out of what
      out of / a smell / a wafting / a rain / good dogs
      bring in the mail / good dogs lay down / i go on

but you can't / stop listening to
redbone / you can't stop
prodding me open / you can't stop
cutting the salt / with sugar
when something / tastes off
your scratch of red / burning mouth
when something / tastes off
you say / do i taste shock
on your breath / and i go on to say
i caught you red-handed

KIMBERLY J. BROWN

Kimberly J. Brown is the author of *The I-35W Bridge Collapse: A Survivor's Account of America's Crumbling Infrastructure* (University of Nebraska Press/Potomac Books). An information technology technical writer, Kimberly studies creative writing in the Hamline MFA program. She lives in Minneapolis with Rachel Anderson, whom she married in 2005.

Twirl, Untwirl

Our first date was at Vera's Café in Uptown where we ordered mochas and lattes. It was probably as awkward and cliché as dates maybe are, save one clumsy game of Trivial Pursuit where Rachel botched the answer to a math question. I had hated math since fourth grade, when—sitting at my grandpa's rolltop desk, feet not touching the floor, trying to do fractions—I knew that I didn't care about numbers at all.

Card in hand, I read, "What's seventy percent of seventy?" I scanned her face for the answer. She stumbled, mumbling to herself. When she settled on a number, I cried, "Wrong! It's forty-nine." She slapped her palm to her forehead. But her poor math delighted me, and I knew then that she was *perfect*.

For our second date, I invited her over to watch *If These Walls Could Talk 2* with some friends. She called to say she might not make it. My heart dropped, but I feigned nonchalance. "Well, another time." She showed up after all, late, but she was there, and I did my best to hide my elation. Months later, Rach confessed she was so nervous, she'd irrationally hoped to get in a car accident—nothing serious, just a little fender bender to get her out of it.

• • •

Today, I call her "wife" for simple and complicated reasons. Simple, because after catastrophe, like surviving the 35W bridge collapse on August 1, 2007, "wife" is the only relationship that people understand, without question. What we'd almost lost was not what others mistakenly reduced us to: "friends."

Almost two years after the collapse, we left home for vacation.

In the Jacuzzi together, I trace invisible lines down her arm like the highways that head north out of the Twin Cities.

Water propels against our feet, pulses the smalls of our backs. We hold. Pull. Close. Closer. Underwater, I skim slippery skin. Over the din of jets, in the heat of the bath, with bubbles crisping in champagne flutes, we canoodle. I feel the safety of her breath by my ear; her lips graze my cheek.

Outside, below slivers of white and blue, the arced horizon draws a line along the top of Lake Superior's white gray. Gulls fly high, low, and dive from view. White flashes against pine trees that shoot to the skies and guard the rocky lakeshore.

I feel her body as if it were new. As if we were new. Here. Now. Ready. Water in constant motion. Later, in the moonlight, our worlds connect. The lofted ceiling is a V; sob the miles logged since collapse, progress made. Fears felt, realized.

We are everything: on this bed, at this lakeshore, in dim light, with my best friend. Bonded, in the most personal way people can be. *Lucky me, lucky us.*

• • •

Complicated is the texture of a life two people make together. Post–bridge collapse, celebrating becomes important in our lives. Ten years after we met, Rachel threw me a surprise anniversary party. She'd planned it for months. She wrote me a love song and performed it before our friends.

The next morning, when I shampooed and shed as I usually do, shorn from my head was a heart! A strand of black hair. Lying damply on my hand, next to ordinary and straight locks—a looped axis and three twists at the stem.

I stood and stared. Stunned. Stupefied. Startled.

I wrestled with chance. Wash it away? Wrest it from my wrist, for savings?

But as soon as I touched a tip to its tendril, it unwound. As hearts do. And was released, as is the nature of chance and happiness. As is fate, luck, and love.

When I gave up the chase, it set on my palm, unbidden. Flowing out of me from my skin. Twirl, untwirl. As hearts do.

Nate Cannon is an award-winning speaker and the author of two books. *Running on a Mind Rewired* has been used to teach about chemical dependency and mental illness. His second memoir, *Dying to Hang with the Boys*, explores the complexities of transition and living with layered identity. Nate holds an MFA from Hamline University.

The Invisible Man

Somewhere in the layers of transition and disability, I lost my sense of belonging. As a transgender man living with bipolar and a progressive neurological illness, I've felt the stigma of mental illness—and of having an invisible disability. Though *dystonia* may sound like an eastern European country, it's actually a neurological condition closely related to Parkinson's disease, caused by a disruption in the mechanism that allows muscles to relax when not in use. It leads to painful spasms and contractions that pull the body into awkward, often uncomfortable postures. Though I've had chest surgery, changed my name and gender marker, and been on T long enough that my gender is never questioned by passersby, it's a sad irony that the only place I have a true cock is in my head.

Dystonia tilts my head. It pulls me to the right, creates limitations, and is both painful and uncomfortable. But unless you know what you're looking for, it's invisible. The same has become true of my being transgender. It's invisible unless I reveal it. Or unless the wrong guy happens to see my small feet pointing the wrong direction under a bathroom stall, the unmistakable sound of a pressurized stream echoing off the water splash.

Back when my gender was seen by others as female, I reached a crossroad where my physical and mental health were suffering due to gender dysphoria. My physicians warned me that my dystonia would mean a long, complicated recovery from gender correction surgery. The dystonia, a result of head trauma and chemical dependency, also altered the wiring of my brain. That made testosterone a scary prospect.

In turn, the trans docs, well respected in the field, weren't sure they wanted to put someone with bipolar disorder, a history of two suicide attempts, multiple brain injuries, and serious chemical dependency on a hormone that could conceivably cause even more emotional fluctuations. Those same docs were hesitant to take a scalpel to my chest for fear it could worsen my neurological condition.

I knew the risks, but they were risks I was willing to take. After all, it was my suicide attempt in December 2011 that caused my partner of ten years to leave our relationship. When I came out to her as trans, it challenged her identity as a lesbian much the way I'd been confusing my own sexual orientation with my gender identity for much of my life.

All the years I spent addicted to chemicals, self-medicating, holding on to the belief that my gender differences could be chalked up to the fact that I was attracted to women were a farce. I was fooling myself. I knew when I was a kid what was right for me. At age five, I asked for what I could then only describe as a "sex change," and it felt simple and natural. When that dysphoria resurfaced as an adult, it felt repulsive and shameful. But over time I realized transition was not a choice. It felt just as urgent and pressing as any drug I'd been addicted to.

In addition to my own psychologist, I saw a gender psychologist early in 2011. "I want my tits chopped off and to start on testosterone," I told him. "I don't want to wait any longer. I'm already thirty."

He scribbled notes furiously and dragged on the process, appointment after appointment. Testosterone wouldn't be an option until I completed at least another six months of gender-specific therapy, and even then, there was no guarantee he'd give me the green light. Meanwhile, insurance would only cover surgery if I had lived "full-time" as a man for a year. I couldn't satisfy that requirement. Even if I had been working a full-time job, I could've risked my safety if I'd presented myself as a man at work when I still looked like a woman.

All of those factors fueled the 2011 suicide attempt that put me in respiratory failure and a subsequent coma. It marked the death of the woman I was and the birth of the man I would become.

Only after nearly losing my life and losing my partner did I realize just how complex a web my identity had woven. With tunnel vision,

I set out in 2012 to transition. I went back to work and put on my best façade to show just how stable I was. The roadblocks and barriers to access I'd encountered prior to the attempt were still there, but I was ready to plow through them.

"I want to transition," I told the same hotshot doc once more. "I want to become a man. I want surgery, testosterone, and to legally change my name and gender marker. I've waited long enough and want to pursue this now."

Still, there were hurdles. In his eyes, my mental health history still necessitated more gender therapy. I knew I wasn't alone. Those of us with mental illness have long faced additional barriers to transition, including being asked to undergo far more psychological treatment.

I'd had enough. I researched and found a different doctor—an ob-gyn with a transgender specialty. After one appointment and a review of my medical notes, I walked out with a prescription for testosterone and support for chest surgery.

It's sad. I had to lose nearly everything before being allowed to move forward with gender transition. But step by step, I figured out my own personal road map to becoming a man.

I started testosterone in July 2012 and began the top-surgery process. Having pursued it before, I knew what questions to ask the insurance company. But the employer-based insurance plan I was now on had an outright policy exclusion, instead of a "full-time living as a man" requirement. I didn't care. I wasn't about to let coverage or money stand between me and my identity. I kept working full-time plus part-time and took out a loan in order to proceed, even though my physical and mental health were challenging my ability to work at all.

That's the tricky part about being trans. We've felt unstable in our identities but been forced to present ourselves to health care professionals as stable to be allowed to move forward with transition. I put on the show, fought through my condition, and got the official seal of stability.

The surgery itself, which was cheaper to have done in Florida than at home in Minnesota, went smoothly. The recovery was not as complicated as the doctors feared, and I was also finding some sense of emotional stability with my testosterone levels. Financially, though, I would remain thousands of dollars in debt for years.

With the main physical piece of the process complete, I turned to the legal side and got my name and gender marker changed two months after surgery, in December 2012. But during the six to eight months when I was actively undergoing this transition process, something strange happened.

I felt I no longer belonged in any of my communities. My lesbian friends backed away from me. So, too, did many of my online friends in the dystonia, mental health, and recovery communities. It was scary. I was raw with emotion from the suicide attempt and breakup, with rejection and abandonment still lurking around every turn.

Perhaps some people may not have approved of my gender. Others may not have understood it. I'll never know. But either way, I found myself feeling just as isolated in the months after I came out to the world in 2012 as I did when I was struggling to come out.

I had to come out publicly. I was wrestling with dysphoria when my first book was published, and reading comments about what an inspiring woman I was only amplified my distress. But the book was written by the woman I was. It deserved to have her name on the cover.

I used social media and a website to promote it. Coming out on those platforms was necessary if I ever wanted to integrate my transgender identity. But for the rest of my life, if I speak of that book—that accomplishment—people will know I was once a woman. Sometimes I don't want to disclose that. Sometimes it's not even safe to do so.

Coming out online in already small subcommunities forever changed the dynamics of my acquaintanceships and readership. Having a book out under my former female name necessitated that I stay out as transgender. I didn't, and still don't, have the option of "going stealth." But it has seemed that people I otherwise connected with based on recovery status or common mental or physical health challenges could no longer relate to me or my story when the trans factor was added in. And the more time went on, the more it became clear to me that I was starting to be perceived as privileged due to visible factors, while the invisible aspects that generated my diversity were becoming just that: invisible.

I started to be viewed as an able-bodied white man with all the privilege in the world. With that, the expectations changed. As a man, I'm expected to be able to lift that heavy bag overhead for a woman on an airplane. Despite the disability others can't see, the societal pressure to "man up" and be strong has caused me to take on tasks such as those that I might have declined, or not been asked to perform, when I was a woman. Just as when I was a kid, I've had to show I can hang with the boys.

It is a curious thing, the complexities of belonging. Sometimes we have to let go not only of societal expectations but of our position within a community to honor our own identities. Only then do we truly seem to find ourselves.

For many of us who are trans, belonging has never quite come naturally. We've been playing the role of the wrongly suited gender for years or, in my and many other cases, decades. Now? I want what anyone else wants. I want the freedom to be myself, to be accepted, to love and be loved for the man I am.

What I've discovered instead is that many people hold a lot of hatred for me just because of who I am. After gay marriage became legal and certain celebrities came out as trans, the backlash began.

I felt it.

Most won't say it, but some in the L and G sections of the LGBT community resist the T's. The T section can be segregated within itself. And many allies have resisted trans folk despite claiming to be accepting. That's not even to mention the rest of the population, who may have palpable disdain for trans persons.

In fact, I've received more hateful feedback, comments, emails, and attacks since 2016 than I did from 2012 to 2015, combined. I did nothing different. I was *less* visible on social media. But the climate had changed. People were talking about gender identity. And I, like many others, became an easy target: from the locker room to the workplace to the doctor's office.

Long before the pushback began, I started to feel the distance. A few online female friends backed away from me as hormones began to change my physical appearance. "My husband doesn't really want me talking to you anymore," I heard from one. When I was an open lesbian, it was perfectly fine for her to talk to me as a friend. I've primarily had female friends as an adult. My intentions were never questioned before transition.

The pushback stretched even into my own community. What few close friends I had prior to transition were primarily lesbians. I lost those friends to transition. One, someone I'd been good friends with for fourteen years, sent me an email in 2012 telling me I was the most amazing person she'd ever met. Then she quoted the Dr. Seuss book *Oh, the Places You'll Go!*

I replied, told her I loved that book, and suggested we get coffee soon.

It was the last I ever heard from her. I tried reaching out again but heard nothing back. I see now her email was a way of saying goodbye. Much the way my ex did, she stressed what an amazing person she thought I was. Then she wished me well on my journey.

What messages we get from media and Facebook alone suggest women and men are supposed to live up to some stereotypical definition of manhood and womanhood. This is true even within the LGBT community, where it seems to be okay to gender bend a bit just so long as your true gender is not questionable. That's when people start to get uncomfortable.

The world, including the internet, can be a hate-filled place. It can segregate and isolate as much as it can help us connect and communicate. It's made transgender people visible, and it's given us a voice, a community, a friend. But when identity gets complicated, it can be hard to see the spoonfuls of love and acceptance through the piles of hate.

Now more than ever, it's crucial that I hold on tight to my identity and embrace who I am. If I speak out, I risk the backlash. But I could also help change lives, change laws, and change statistics. If I allow the world to silence me, I put myself at significant risk of becoming nothing more than what I've always feared: a suicide stat.

Oh, the lengths we go, the prices we pay, and the risks we must take to be who we are.

ANTHONY CEBALLOS

Anthony Ceballos received his BFA from Hamline University in St. Paul. In 2016 he was selected to be a Loft Literary Center Mentor Series mentee. His poetry has been featured in *Yellow Medicine Review, Midway Journal, Sleet, Writers Resist,* and *Great River Review*. He can be found penning staff recommendations at Birchbark Books in Minneapolis.

Ink Flow

Through my veins
ink flows, when it breaks
                    from my skin,
            pours onto paper,
                    it is not for you.

When each word wrapped   in saliva
                        throws itself from the edge
                                    of my tongue,
                    make no mistake,
                            it's not your arms
                    they're aiming for.

        Not your ears,
            not your eyes, my syllables
                will not drown in a white
        sea, white foam, white space overwhelms
    my brown vernacular.

These lines are not for you,
        I am not your muse.
                My cadence is not
                        a spell to make you
            feel good, feel God, rid your
                        homesickness, your
                need to be cultured.

These words
are a taste for your tongue, glass cutting
           your gums, chipping your teeth,

       this is not an act of kindness,
              act of love,
                     it is the breath of revolution
       from my lungs, a different
kind of acid
       from every chamber
              of my heart.

Sweetest Nothing

Split my tongue   use the sharp
                   end   of your heart,
     watch my
             blood,   my
             "I love yous,"   fall
against your chest,
     stain your shirt,
          brown and red
     stain
             where my heart should be,

     fill the hole
          with alcohol,   old friend,
     family member   nobody wanted,

              infected

tongue burns on contact, get me

          away from my body, this body
              you held,

     this body
        you said you loved,   emptied,
          hollowed, sweet nothing on the wind,

     just that, nothing
          tastes so sweet, scent
     of coconut and cheap
     cologne, pour another

    glass of "I'll be alright,"
        courage,
   phony,

help   me

        press on, this   broken

                body even

I have trouble   loving sometimes,   why

                why would you love me any less?

Stephanie Chrismon received an MFA from Hamline University and was a 2016–17 Loft Mentor Series winner in creative nonfiction and a 2015 Givens Foundation Emerging Writers' Mentor Program fellow. Her writing has appeared in *The Root,* and her novel *Bright City* (under the name dc edwards) was published in 2017.

Let the Church Say Amen

While waiting to meet the Lord at Saint Peter's pearly gates, Aiesha anticipated her turn to answer the Archangel Michael's question, "If you could do anything on Earth, what would it be?"

Well, of course, many souls on line asked for second chances and riches. And with the snap of his manicured fingers they disappeared, then reappeared even faster, never once seeming much different from when they originally left. So Aiesha realized quickly that going back to redo everything wasn't much of an option. The semi she slammed her Mercedes into had snapped her head clean off. And frankly, she'd won the lottery a couple of times and it wasn't a picnic—folks always had their hands out. So when Michael got to her, his glistening, honey-colored eyes taking in her pink T-shirt and jeans that hugged her curves, she knew exactly what she wanted to do.

"So, if you could go back and do anything, what would it be?"

"I want to give a toast at my wedding."

Michael's perfectly arched eyebrow jerked upward as his full, thick lips formed a dazzling smile.

"This I have to see."

The year was 1990. Aiesha was marrying her high school sweetheart, Phillip Bell III. Aiesha and Michael were a sight to see. Michael in his high-waisted, double-pleated navy linen pants with the matching three-quarter-length suit coat. And her in a matching navy cinched and belted calf-length skirt with shoulder pads and hoop earrings. They looked horribly stunning.

"Now don't get any ideas; we are only here until you do your toast, which will be after your husband's brother rambles on about marrying beneath him."

Aiesha followed Michael's lead as they moved toward the front of the Prince Hall Mason Lodge #6 to sit at the table right in front of the head table.

Aiesha noticed that no one in the hall recognized her. But, she thought, *why would they?* She had a head full of braids and just a few wrinkles creasing her sepia-toned skin. She was about fifty pounds heavier than her younger self. A couple of children and depressive eating helped with that. She also moved differently. These days she glided into every room. Her younger self usually stumbled or slinked, eager to not be seen. In the early days of their relationship, Phillip managed to take up most of the air in any room he entered. She had simply been happy he noticed her.

She looked around the large hall and scoffed at the tasteless decorations. Everything was either wine- or pearl-colored; the tablecloths, the centerpieces, the bridesmaids' dresses, the groomsmen's boutonnieres. It was as if no expense of bad taste was spared. She remembered sitting at her mother's table being shown patterns and colors and textures and fed pastries and crab cakes and chicken and fish until she thought she'd vomit up the wedding that her mother always wanted.

She glanced at her younger self, knowing that fake smile she had plastered on her face would have her cheeks hurting for a week after. She watched her younger self attempting to ignore Phillip flirting with a beautiful ebony sista, the ex-girlfriend he'd insisted attend. Her resolve grew stronger.

They sat through five speakers before Andrew, Phillip's brother, drunkenly slurred through his speech. Aiesha watched her younger self sink back into her seat as each potshot landed to laughter from Phillip. She could tell most people thought his words were just a friendly roast from her new brother-in-law. But Aiesha knew he meant every word. He spent all of high school hitting on her. And she spent all her time turning him down. When Phillip told his family they were engaged, Andrew got Phillip drunk and sicced Vanessa Jenkins on him. Vanessa Jenkins: pretty, light-skinned, blue-eyed, big-assed Vanessa Jenkins. Phillip begged for three months before Aiesha could forgive him for his indiscretion.

She barely heard Andrew's last word when Michael nudged her under the table.

"Showtime, sista girl, and make it good," he whispered, placing an ebony hand on hers.

She took a swig of champagne, then stepped forward.

"Well, my dear Aiesha, some would say you got yourself into a whole world of mess. Won't you celebrate with me what seems to be the last day you get to be you.

"You see, you a tidy slaughter. Like a lamb headed toward its maker.

"Yes, the Bells love them some obedient, submissive lil' black girls who listen to their elders and husbands and breed. And you will breed, oh yes, you will. In between the two miscarriages and the one abortion, you'll have yourself a couple of kids. A boy and a girl . . . *all. at. once.* And they, the ungrateful entitled little Bell clones, will drive you nuts. And as you know by now, Phillip isn't made for working. Oh, he can make a dollar. But he ain't trying to make a home. He knows how to keep the bed rocking, though; that's one thing you can say. Too bad your bed ain't the only one he rocks in. He can't help it, though; he got those rolling-stone ways from his daddy.

"Look around the room: don't some of these people look more like brothers and sisters than cousins to you?

"Ah, baby girl, if only you knew your potential at nineteen the way you'll know it at damn near forty. But by then, you'll think it's a little too late. And you'll be on your way to another bar, to meet another man to have just one drink to put your mind at rest, and you'll find permanent rest underneath a semi.

"So what I say to you is this: Love your flesh, love your hands, love your neck, and love your head, 'cause in twenty years, when you'll think you've had just about enough, it'll come clean off."

Ms. Robinson

When I was sixteen I fell in love with my mother's best friend. Jacqueline was short and roundish. In her tailored suits, her tiny black sports car, she had a quiet confidence I admired. At the same time I was falling for Jacqueline, I was dating an angry young man from my church youth group who drove a black Buick and always listened to Public Enemy at screeching-high volumes. Andrew was eighteen and a virgin. His grandmother, who raised him, had hoped he would become a minister. Andrew was mostly a polite kid, hands-off. He was just as nervous about sex as I was.

Even though his grandmother told him once that I seemed a bit tainted, he rebelled by dating me, the awkward girl in the youth group who was rumored to be a lesbian.

He'd kissed only one girl in his life before me, so until I showed him how to relax his lips and pull in his tongue, his kisses were sloppy and wet. Still, we never really got past first base; sometimes he would fumble with the hooks on my bra, but he would never undo the buttons on my jeans. I felt safe with him.

One night, though, he decided we weren't going to youth group. He pulled off onto a dark, secluded street. I wasn't in the mood to make out. The week before he'd chatted eagerly about maybe in a couple of years we could probably get engaged. That conversation made me ill. Since then, I'd been thinking about breaking up with him. I felt guilty that whenever I was making out with him I was thinking about Jacqueline. How could he possibly want to marry me?

When we pulled over, the only noise was his tape player blasting Public Enemy. The squeal and pounding 808 of "Rebel without a Pause" filled the space between us. Back then, I liked to pretend his silence was mysterious. But I knew we had nothing in common. He didn't like to read; he didn't like school. He didn't have much to say about anything except music. So we often sat in silence while I waited for him to make an awkward move. Once when I tried to initiate, he pushed me away and sneered that good girls don't do that. So I waited until he put his hand between my legs and began to kiss my neck. I stared out the window, watching the lights on a porch twenty feet away.

"Let's get in the back," he whispered.

This moment started out as it always did: me on top, us kissing frantically as he slipped his hands either under my shirt or down the back of my pants, but over the panties. After twenty minutes of this, he lifted me off him and sat up.

"I want you to suck me off."

"Ummm, excuse me?"

He unzipped his pants and pulled it out. I could feel the heat coming from his pants before he pulled my hand onto it. He guided my hand up and down; it was already slick, and I watched him lean his head back; his eyes rolled up and then closed in ecstasy. Then he wrapped one hand behind my neck and pushed my head down until my lips touched the salty tip of his penis.

"Taste it," he insisted.

I opened my mouth and he guided it in. Of course, I gagged, but he ignored it, moving in and out, using my mouth for a pumping station. I remember thinking, "I'm done with this fool." It was over. After only a minute, which seemed like an eternity, he pushed me back and used his own hand to climax. He abruptly climbed over the armrest and plopped in the driver's seat.

"We can't see each other anymore," he said.

"I know."

"You hungry?"

"Yes."

He drove to White Castle, and we ate in the parking lot. No music; no conversation.

That weekend my parents decided to go to a concert out of town, and since my brothers were staying with friends, they sent me to stay with Jacqueline. I loved her apartment. It was modern and sleek, with metal and wood everywhere. I was most fascinated by her huge, king-size sleigh bed, which she always covered in starched white linens. Whenever I stayed, I'd put my stuff in a cubby she'd built into the wall, and I'd sleep on the foldout couch. I always wondered how it would feel to sleep in that bed. Her apartment smelled like fresh cotton and cinnamon. My parents weren't keen on horror movies, but

Jacqueline and I bonded over being frightened by beasties whenever I'd spend the night.

She'd planned the perfect movie night: *Halloween* on laser disk and pizza from our favorite restaurant. Still, my evening with Andrew played over in my head like a broken tape. I'd trusted Jacqueline with my thoughts before, but this was real. I had a nagging feeling in my stomach that she might hate me if she knew my secret. But I had to talk about it.

"Can I ask you a question?" I asked, between bites of pizza.

"Of course."

"Do you have a boyfriend?"

I remember her smile, the same smile I'd give over the years when people would ask me that same question. It was a smile that said, "I know the answer to a secret."

"No."

"I have one."

"Oh, what's his name?"

"Andrew."

"What's he like?"

"I don't know."

"Nicole, he's your boyfriend; what do you mean you don't know?"

"I don't know; he's quiet and we don't talk much."

"Then how is he your boyfriend?"

"I don't know."

"Nicole you know I am not a fan of 'I don't know.' You know exactly what you want to say. You have your words; use them."

"I've seen his penis."

"That doesn't exactly make you his girlfriend."

"I touched it. I think I gave him a blow job."

I was looking down at my plate, pulling the pepperoni off the crust, separating the black olives, my favorite, from the cheese, adding them to the pile that I always saved for later. I trusted this woman and I waited to be disappointed. I waited for her to give me flak about my secret. I didn't want her to hate me or be disgusted by me. I was embarrassed. The thought of her rejecting me darted through my mind, and I felt my face growing hotter.

"You think you did or you know you did?"

"I know I did."

I avoided her intense, chestnut-colored eyes.

"Why did you do it?"

"I mean, he wanted to, and well . . . I guess I felt like I didn't really have a choice."

"So he forced you?"

"No, he's nice."

"Do you love him?"

"No, I like him. But we don't really have anything in common. He likes this loud song that he plays all the time, and he has a car. He's going to be a minister someday."

"Interesting," she said.

Jacqueline moved closer to me and brushed her hand through my long, shaggy hair. I looked up at her and smiled. She kissed my forehead. The butterflies raged in my stomach, and for minutes I could still feel the soft, light wetness of her lips against my skin.

We spent the evening with her French-braiding my hair, watching the news, and then settling in to watch *Halloween*. I couldn't concentrate on the movie, though. At the scary moments, she pulled me close, wrapping her arms around me, hugging me tighter. At other moments, she absently ran her hand over the freshly tightened braids. When she finally excused herself to get ready for bed, I felt like I couldn't breathe. I just wanted to stop being turned on by her touch.

"See you in the morning, sweetie," she said from her doorway as she gently closed the doors.

The doors to her bedroom were glass and wood, but the glass was thick and wavy. If you were looking into her bedroom, you could see movement but not straight through. I sat up on the made-up couch bed for an hour, staring at the shadow of her changing clothes, then reading, and when the light finally went off, I breathed a sigh of relief and tried to sleep.

A couple of hours later, I sat up suddenly with a scream caught in my throat. For years, I'd had the same dream. I was being chased down the hallway of a dormitory; maggots crawled on the women I passed by, and for some reason, I could not get away. I never looked back, but the hallway was an all-consuming darkness, and just as I thought I was getting to a door, I would fall into a pit of barbed wire and be sliced over and over.

"Nicole, are you okay?" Jacqueline called from the other room.

"Yep, just a nightmare."

"Come get in bed with me, then."

"I'm okay."

"Don't be silly, c'mon."

In the dark, the white accents of her bedroom glowed against the moonlight that filtered through the bay window opposite her bed. I could see the skyline of the city in the near distance. She pulled back the covers and allowed me to sink into the bed, putting her arms around me so that my head could rest on her chest.

"Thanks," I said, my mind begging my heartbeat to slow down.

"I hate nightmares. Was it the movie?"

"No."

"Are you worried I won't keep your secret?"

"A little."

"Why would I tell that?"

"Because you should."

"Do you want me to, though?"

"No."

"Then I won't."

She held up my chin and I could see the sincerity in her eyes, and for whatever reason I took a chance. I pressed my lips to hers, positioning my hand to the nape of her neck. We kissed. I allowed my hands to wander across her body from her shoulders to her breasts to her hips and thighs. Her body felt familiar, warm and soft. Her lips were tender and sweet; we allowed our tongues to linger against one another, taking in each other's breath, as I slid on top of her, pushing her gown up above her thighs. My fingers slipped inside of her and pressed into her wet warmth.

"Nicole," she whispered in a husky, lust-filled voice as her nails gently scraped across my back.

I've spent my life replaying that scene with different women, like a heroin addict chasing that first euphoric feeling when I tasted the sweat on her neck, listened to her moans—and the moment she shook and trembled, pulling my fingers out but me closer to her, and the salty flavor of her tears as we made love again, slower and more intentionally.

When I woke up the next day, I reached for her, but she wasn't there. I figured she went out for breakfast like she often did when I stayed over. I inhaled her musky and thick scent on my fingers before taking a shower. I felt light and expectant. I naively fantasized about our relationship, one that required secrecy until I turned eighteen, and then we could be openly together.

After my shower, I noticed the note she left on the dresser.

Nicole,
I had to go out. Will be back later so go ahead and go home.
Lock the front door.
Later,
Jacqueline

A month later, over a game of spades with friends, my stepdad and mom were talking about Jacqueline. In my household, there was a rule about being a kid around grown-ups: If you wanted to hear the conversation, you shut the fuck up. I was good at that. I sat in the corner with one of the books that Jacqueline had given me, intent on hearing about her. Since she lived in walking distance, I'd gone by her apartment a couple of times after school and called when I could, but there'd never been an answer. I thought about writing her a letter, but I worried about someone finding it.

"Yeah, that chick was trying to move in on my woman," my step-dad said as he sipped a beer and played a card.

"Baby, she did not want me," my mom laughed, throwing down her card, then taking a drink from her tumbler of Hennessy.

"Girl, yes, she did! You didn't know about Miss Thang," the woman with the crooked blonde wig squealed.

"Awww, yeah, bruh, everybody knows about Jackie May; that girl's been a dyke since pharaoh was a boy," said the man with the Jheri curl, the wetness from the activator saturating his already stained burgundy silk shirt as he threw down his card.

"Well, she never wanted me. She's getting married," my mother said, taking another swig.

"That marriage is bogus; she don't want that nigga," my stepdad said, hitting the table with his card.

"Yeah, girl, that fool she's marrying is sugar sweet, too."

"Yeah, he's gayer than a sissy with a bag full of dicks."

"Whew, that is sweet!" laughed my stepdad.

I remember slinking out of the room and up to my bedroom. I took out the note she'd left for me the day after and stared at it. I thought I'd never want to love anyone ever if the pain was even half as bad as it was that night. I had stopped believing in God several years before, but that night I prayed, prayed to be relieved of the pain that threatened to crush my heart.

The next morning as I helped my mother clean the living room and kitchen, we listened to the *Love Express,* my stepdad's gospel radio show. My mother's clear, soulful soprano filled the room as she sang along with all the songs.

"Oh, that reminds me, Jackie wanted me to tell you to have a good rest of the summer."

"Really?"

"Yeah, you know she's going on her honeymoon, and her and Robert won't be moving back here. They're going to Atlanta."

"Oh, that's too bad."

"Yeah, that's my girl. I'm gonna miss her."

"Me, too."

"She also wanted me to give you some books, but I left them at work. I'll pick them up tomorrow."

"Okay."

"She also said to tell you that she loves you and will miss you."

I stopped cleaning and walked over to the window, watching the neighborhood kids playing tag in the street and hanging out on their porches, hip-hop music blaring from stereos. The day was warm but comfortable, and a slight, cool breeze ran through the trees. It was the perfect summer day. I sprayed some more lemon Pledge on my rag and began to clean the dust off the bookshelf.

"I love her, too."

JAMES CIHLAR

James Cihlar's books include *The Shadowgraph, Rancho Nostalgia,* and *Undoing.* His chapbooks are *A Conversation with My Imaginary Daughter* and *Metaphysical Bailout.* His writing has appeared in *The American Poetry Review, The Threepenny Review, Lambda Literary Review, Prairie Schooner, Nimrod,* and *Smartish Pace.*

Double Indemnity

If your lipstick smears, the makeup man will fix it.
That's his job. We all have jobs.
Don't teach me, help me.

Stand still while centuries move around you.
You try not to age, but sometimes it's unavoidable.
With every role, you grow another skin.

If you're going to practice making decisions,
you'll need to be able to change your mind.
It's what the script calls for.

Maybe you didn't know at the time
you were in the right place. The way they lit the set,
the moves, the business, the atmosphere,

made it easy for you to slip into your role,
to see your hand on the banister, the bracelet on your ankle.
All you ask is to appear in the last fifteen minutes,

your face in multiples around you.
If you are the watcher and the watched,
then you must be in every movie ever seen.

As the filming wraps, you think, *I hope she'll be okay.*
You miss people before they are gone.
Sometimes, when you talk to yourself, you answer, *yes, me too.*

Melodrama

Act I.

A woman is alone in a room in a city.
Her room is in a skyscraper.
The windows are outsized,
and the view is important.

Her hair is carefully disheveled
or tightly coiffed.
She has an air of professionalism,
or an air of desperation.

She knows a dangerous secret.
Either no one will believe her
or she won't admit it to herself.
A stranger tries to convince her

or her husband tries to tell her
that it's all in her head.
She slowly begins to believe him.
She furiously refuses to believe him.

The phone rings multiple times
She answers it and shudders.
She answers it and screams.
Someone is outside the window.

Act II.

She stumbles to him in her nightgown.
She spies on him through binoculars.
He is Sigmund Freud,
playing a shell game.

She has to guess which cup hides the coin.
He is Adolf Hitler,
holding a puppy.
She has to entice the dog away from him.

They end up going to court over custody
of the dog.
Hitler's lawyer, Joe McCarthy,
subpoenas her deceased parents.

Freud dons a snood and a pencil skirt
to masquerade as her mother.
Hitler testifies
that he's her real father.

The judge commits her to a sanitarium.
Still alive, she is put in an open casket
and given shock treatment.
The dog is run over by a car.

Act III.

She falls in love with her doctor.
He discovers she has a terminal disease
without a name. She will be pretty
until the day she dies. Snow will fall

outside the window on that day.
But before then, the doctor's
children disapprove of their romance,
so she breaks up with him.

He releases her from the sanitarium
and she walks in the middle of the street,
her shoulder pads backlit by the sun,
never to see him again.

Then her husband reveals he is the stranger,
Hitler, and Freud rolled into one,
and he is the one who ran over the dog.
He chases her into a skyscraper.

They climb endless flights of stairs.
When he charges toward her at the top
she dodges and he spirals to the pavement.
The little dog limps into her arms.

The Furies

When Walter Huston wrestles a calf
out of the mud in Anthony Mann's

The Furies, while Barbara Stanwyck
throws back her head and laughs,

it's the most honest image in Hollywood.
Our feelings are a blast of music.

Love and lust are *blam, blam, blam.*
1950 hated the world for not being pretty.

When Stanwyck casts aside pearls
for diamonds, it changes the air

in the theater. When she rides her horse
to the squatter's fort

and warns her Mexican lover,
she wrings the neck of eloquence.

You'd think the happiest answer
would be transposing an old world

problem to the new. But Utopia
doesn't last here either.

Stanwyck doesn't like what they've done
with her image, the myth of the West,

taken from the Golden Age to Iron. It's funny
how they think it's theirs,

when she knows it's hers.
Mann saw the pretty in the ugly.

Sometimes winning is just outliving.
Even God is not above the body.

Venus de Mars, leader of the glam-punk/trans band Venus de Mars & All The Pretty Horses, is a recipient of both the McKnight Multidisciplinary Artist and the Bush Artist Support fellowships, a core artist from the 1980s' Rifle Sport Alternative Art Gallery, and, along with her wife, the subject of the rock-doc *Venus of Mars* (2004).

Kite

May 1970. Duluth. 53rd and Norwood.

He's insists that I *am* a girl. I tell him that no, I'm not, but he insists. He adds that his brother says so and I can see he is getting angry with me, so I don't argue anymore, or I lessen my argument because he is younger than me. Maybe two years younger, which would make him maybe eight years old, and I can tell I may not be able to dissuade him and I really don't want to meet his brother, so I stop talking and instead shift my focus to the kite I'm flying now so high in the air that I can barely see it.

I am older and wiser than him anyway. And taller. Like a foot taller. He takes my silence as confirmation that indeed I *was* just fooling him, and now that he's won the argument, he also turns his attention to the kite, or actually to why I'm holding a stick with string tied around it. And I explain that I'm flying a kite, and he says no I'm not because he can't see it, but he's still curious as to why the string looks as if it's going into the air. I tell him to follow the string up as far as he can see and then to look really carefully, and finally he does see the kite and he becomes absorbed by it and asks how I got it up there so high and if I might let *him* hold the stick with the string tied around it, and I say okay.

I hand it to him and say to be careful not to let go. He is amazed at how much the kite pulls against his grasp, and then I take it back.

It's misting and cool and muggy out. The sky is gray and clouds drift. I am wearing my jeans and tennies and my gray zipper sweatshirt jacket with its pointy hood up, and I'm wearing nothing underneath it because it's so muggy. And also because of that I have the zipper unzipped down to mid-chest and I can see this boy I don't know look again at my thin, hairless chest and now I understand maybe why he's confused. And maybe I feel kind of okay with his confusion.

Yes, I am okay with his confusion.

I find myself wishing he is right and that I am just pretending, but now his focus has shifted and he's more interested in the kite than me and asks all the questions he can think of.

So I answer as best I can. I tell him how I built it and how I run to get it to go into the air. I tell him I run for two blocks to do it, then walk back a block to where I am now with the kite way up in the air. And then I explain how if I time my running and raise it higher and higher by letting out string and running again if it begins to drop, eventually I can get it high enough, like I have today, that it never drops and the wind never quits and I can just stand and hold the stick with the string for as long as I want.

I see he has lost track of what I'm telling him and now wants to leave, so he waves goodbye and runs down the avenue, dodging puddles as he goes, calling back once to ask if I'll be here tomorrow and I say I don't know and he waves again, turns, and is gone.

Mist beads on my hands and face.

I am glad I'm alone again. I'm glad his brother didn't follow him. And I'm glad no one who knows me calls for me. Calls to ruin this accidental agreement which this boy I don't know and I have made, and as I watch the tiny kite way up in the sky I remember Max from last summer. The other boy I don't know. The one who last year, as I am playing with other boys at Todd's house, arrives from down another street wearing a dress. None of us knows him. He asks if he can join us and Todd or someone says yes.

And someone else asks what his name is and he tells us it's Max and to never mind that he's wearing a dress because he doesn't want to but his mom makes him wear it even though he's a boy.

And then I want to be Max's friend. And I wonder why Max's mother would make him wear a dress, and I wish my mother would make me wear a dress, and then someone whispers in my ear that Max isn't really a boy. He whispers that she's just some girl from a few blocks away and that he's seen her before and her name isn't Max but he doesn't know her real name. He tells me that they always play the same game with her and I should join them in playing it because it's a trick on her. Then he warns me not to ruin anything. And I don't know these boys but I know Todd from school, and I had only come up this far along Glendale Street to see him, not everyone else, and I'm unsure as to what I should do but the game is starting and I am being pulled in.

Kevin, I think, one of the maybe six boys in Todd's yard, calls to line up for the game. This other boy, the whispering one, quietly explains the rules. It involves each boy back-crawling between a single standing boy's spread-apart legs. A fast-moving, nonstop, snakelike circle of ground-level, back-shuttling, group movement. A quick up and run, then drop and crawl. An elbow-digging, heel-kicking, fast-moving circle of nine-year-olds.

I'd never heard of this made-up game before and I'm feeling vaguely uncomfortable and I wish Todd had been here alone instead of with all these boys I don't know, but I still want to be Max's friend now so I stay anyway. This whispering boy finishes with a final explanation: He points out this is how we can all see Max's underwear, though he doesn't say *Max's underwear*, instead he says *her underwear*, but I'm still thinking of her as Max. And maybe Max is like me I think. And maybe after the game Max and I can talk.

And just then Kevin calls "go," and boys begin to drop, including Max. All back-crawling crazy except for the standing spread-leg boy. Through his legs goes a squirming line of slowly shifting, sideways kicking, elbow digging boys on backs. A slip-side slow shuttle circle, shifting steadily across the yard like a circular, gigantic, many-bodied, back-wiggling human centipede, steadily flipping tall as each last boy, finishing, stands to replace the previous standing one, who now runs around to drop again and joins the back-sliding, many-boy snake. And now it's Max's turn to stand and so he does with legs apart and the snake slows down and I am pulled by the whispering boy onto the ground to join the snake through Max's legs and from the street someone calls sharply, "Mary." And then calls "Mary" again more angrily than before. Mom-voice angry. An adult is calling from the window of a car now stopped in front of Todd's yard and all the boys get up and run except me and Max. And I stand up cuz Max is already standing and I feel dumb laying on the grass alone. And Max is upset because his mom has ruined everything. I can tell. He looks at me and says something like it's my mom again, and gives me an exasperated look like he really hates this, and then gets into the car because Max's mom is insisting he does.

Then Max's mom looks at me. I can tell she's really angry. She tells me that I should be ashamed and then drives away with Max inside.

The whisper boy walks over from behind Todd's house and wonders aloud why I didn't run. And then he guesses, also aloud, that it must be because I'm so stupid, and he continues with his out-loud wondering that maybe I might be as stupid as Max, only he doesn't call him Max, he calls him that crazy girl.

And I walk home alone. And I never see Max again.

And now as I stand here at 53rd and Norwood a year later holding a stick with a string tied around it, the mist has turned to rain. I put the stick on the ground and step on it. I grab the string with my two hands and while I stay stepping on the stick I break the string away. I hold it awhile as the kite tugs at my grasp, and then, as the rain really starts to pour, I let the string go.

Late Night

Summer 1981
Duluth
2 AM

I fashion and file a small, flat ring. Its diameter is half an inch. Its thickness, one-sixteenth. Its flatness, the result of crafting a sheet of brass using a jeweler's saw. If it were copper, it would appear as if a penny has had its center drilled out with a gap just enough for a small pinch of skin. At this gap are the ends. The first, a filed and sand-smoothed taper, which quickly forms a short, stubby, needle-prick point. Across is the other. A flat-square end finish. Its surface is brushed, not polished. Lacking this tool, I use emery cloth to smooth its sharp filings instead. Its saw-jag edge.

I stay up late nights. I rehearse with my band, dream of a life on-stage, and eventually I fall asleep. I work early evenings pumping gas at the Clark station on the corner lot next to my apartment. My second-level, 1930s, maple-floored, oak-trimmed, lath-and-plaster, condemned apartment, which extends front to back along the west side of this block-long, three-level, old world, Duluth, Minnesota, brownstone. I pay one hundred and twenty-five dollars a month rent. Under the table. An agreement with the owner. In exchange, I manage all my own apartment repairs without assistance. My west-facing windows overlook the Clark station. Overlook the corner. Overlook the cars pulling in and driving out. When I finish work, my windows take the station's tall white fluorescents. Let them illuminate my walls from sunset till station close. Then as the fluorescents are switched off, mercury-orange from the corner streetlights dims in to replace them. And after a long time, I drift-fall asleep in their cold, golden glow.

I awake near noon, at the sound of pitched pebbles. As they catch on my window, thrown up by my coworkers. And my day/nights repeat.

Tonight I am holding my finished brass ring and I review my plan:

FIRST, position the stub-point needle end on my tiny pinch of skin. Complete the piercing by hand-pushing it hard through.

SECOND, blunt the point, once complete. Use a small file.
THIRD, close the gap with pliers.
FOURTH, clean and care for the wound until skin heals around brass.

I've taken a tray of ice cubes and set it next to me. Notice how the condensation builds along the tray sides. How it drips onto the tabletop.

I twist-crack the tray, loose the cubes, and begin icing a small area of skin just at the back of my scrotum. Just where it attaches to my body. I ice it for half an hour. I drink beer to blur hesitation. I believe pain will be managed.

I hate my scrotum, my penis, my maleness, myself.
My thoughts of suicide are forgotten as I imagine a piercing success.

I recall a nude image from a porn magazine. A woman with a
    piercing near this same body location, except she has no penis,
    no scrotum, no maleness.
I am struck by her beauty.
I am struck by the piercing. Its uniqueness.
I am struck by our difference.
And a depth in my stomach clenches as I recall. Like a gentle black
    hole soft-pulling at my insides, slow and steady.
Deep center.
A pull steady into sadness, like empty gathers into storm.
But my piercing will break this storm.
Its sharpness will tear this sadness.
Its success will destroy this slow-pull of bad.
My piercing will dominate.
Overtake my penis.
Overtake my scrotum.
Replace them both.
And it will make me powerful. Whole. Fearless.
I will claim strength through endurance.
I will conquer my shame. My self-hatred. My all.
And my heart—beats—a rhythm. Blank and presence.

Like a month previous. Like when I buy this new LP.
This *"Flowers of Romance."*
This "Public Image Ltd."
A music so different from anything I've heard.
I walk to the London Road new-and-used record store.
Two blocks east and three blocks south.
Buy this new vinyl.
Open windows back home.
Summer brightness heats the air.
I tear the wrapped plastic.
Slide out the black disk.
Push it flat on the platter.
Shaft pressed through its heart.
Place the needle. Twist the knob.
Lie on the maple-wood smoothness.
The sparse floor of my apartment.
Lie in a pool of sun and blood-red blackness.
Vessels glow on eyelids shut.
Heart rhythm through tiny veins.
My arms stretch toward walls.
Like a crucifixion.

And this music opens a universe.
And fuck the radio playlist. Fuck its industry standard.
My head on the floor.
My brain between speakers.

I follow the drums. Touch the edge of measured time. Caress at
bass notes as they push me back. As they knock me sideways. And I
stumble and catch. A sharpness of tone.

where a voice now threads
where I am buried alive
where I am buried gone
and I am buried disappeared

and I carve this dark
as it hides my secret fear
my desire for impossible
my hours of self-hate

but I am strong enough to weep
and so I cut flesh as I dream
and so I blank thought when I wake

and now it's dark and it's late
and with a leg over armrest
and a mirror set crooked

I place smooth-filed ring
this sharp needle-point stub
against tightly pinched skin
as I press left thumb and first finger

so cold to the touch
press tight at the pinch
till it's all blood-gone pale
till it's all nerve-block white

feel the melted ice frozen
feel the breath when I breathe
feel the stop when I wait
feel the pain when I push

pierce past the skin surface
blood covers my fingertips
they slip when I push
and I slip with my touch

readjust past the warmth
readjust past the wet.
readjust past the sweat
and the iron smell of it all

and my nerves come alive

a recognition of source

and my grip slips again

leaving point lodged in deep
and the pain is like fire
as the blood rushes back.
and I can't push the exit

can't pierce the other side
and my mind bursts open
I must get it through
and I make myself a promise

I will love all my body
I will embrace this small jewel
and my gender will diminish
and a wholeness renew

and I try one more time
and again
again
again

again

but my finger's grip fails
and my skin-pinch is lost
old blood sticks like honey
new blood slips like paste

and here the ring hangs
half in skin and half not through
and I'm goddamned-flat
and I'm god-fucking-done

and so I free the damn thing
throw it *violent* away
and I clean the half-piercing
let the alcohol sting

and my thoughts all dull-drift
and I end all this shit
as I know I am a man
and insane to think other

And I sleep hard through the night.
Through a lifetime and sweat.

And tomorrow I grasp, at a small razor's edge. I see hell in a mirror. And I cut through my long hair. Holding ends as I saw. I watch chunks of it spill. And it takes fifteen minutes. Till all my skull is gone ragged.
   Till the sink is messed-full. And I weep at my terror.
   This is me.

This is me.

JAY OWEN EISENBERG

Jay Owen Eisenberg is a Minneapolis-based actor, writer, director, and arts educator. He was the recipient of a 2017 Minnesota State Arts Board Artist Initiative Grant for his solo show, *Big Old Rock*. Jay earned his BFA from New York University Tisch School of the Arts. As a writer, he is represented by Alloy Entertainment.

Entomologist

1.

For someone who claims to love insects,
what I think I mean is:
I'm fond of them
when they show up in
(what I perceive as)
the right place
at the right time.
Which is, perhaps,
the same way I feel about
cayenne pepper,
knock-knock jokes,
and love.

2.

I'll be honest, now:
I killed one, the other night.
This one had an injured wing,
and a body heavy enough
to make a small sound
when it fell to the floor.
I do not think it was its life
that I found so offensive,
but its inevitable, approaching death,
and the sound of its fate, sealed.
The sound of it trying and failing,

and trying and failing,
and trying and failing
to get off the ground,
audible suffering in action,
slow and repetitive and just not-silent enough.
I crushed it between some envelopes,
the same envelopes I use
for handwritten letters
and rent checks.
I have not yet checked to see
what it looks like, now.
But have you ever found yourself trying and failing,
and trying and failing,
and trying and failing,
to say something you've been meaning to say,
and then, finally, you just
say it?
I bet it's kind of like that.

3.

I'm sorry to say, I liked this one simply because
it was pretty and it kept me company.
Green and glistening, it joined me at my first mile,
stayed with me as I biked ten more.
Perched on my shoulder, and then my neck,
a small angel, or devil, or talking conscience,
but no, sweeter than that, more like
the sound of his breath in your ear.
It's true: I've always been a fool
for the beautiful ones.

4.

She told me they poured out of the nectarine.
I mean, like, they suddenly appeared.
I mean, like, they weren't there and then they were.
Like a sinkhole.
Like a Magic Eye painting.
Like a forgotten memory, resurfacing.

5.

Consider, age 4, you watch your father step on ants,
and as you witness his anger, you learn to conceal yours.
Consider, age 10, you accidentally kill a fruit fly
between your thumb and pointer finger, and you sob.
Consider, age 22, you're bitten by a tick,
and your body hasn't been the same since.
Consider, age 27, you find out he saved a bee's life,
and your heart writes a note to itself:
"Remember this."

6.

For someone who claims to love insects,
what I think I mean is:
I'm fond of using their life cycles
as a means of measuring
the passage of time.
Measure hardship in terms of growth for once,
rather than in terms of loss,
as I am usually prone to do.
Tell myself that this rough patch
might only be as long as a ladybug's larval stage,
or a monarch's migration.

Granite Falls, Minnesota

I would more or less
prefer to be the world's
oldest granite
on the side of the road
in western Minnesota.
The world's oldest granite
has 3.8 billion years to its name and is
a reasonably good photo opportunity and is
mildly famous
in the minds of certain geologists
and certain geology enthusiasts.
It's not that I want
to be old,
photogenic,
or famous,
though I wouldn't object
to being one or more of those things
at some point in my life.
I mean, it would be nice to be
a place where
you could rest,
if you were able to relax your body
into my ridges
and find unexpected softness,
likened to lichen,
instead
of whatever
unpleasant sensation it was
for which you'd been
bracing.
I've been there,
too,
always on the edge of my seat, with
boots laced up and keys in hand,

ready to bolt at the first sign
of my house
or my heart
on fire.
It's not that I want
to be perfect,
patient,
or even good,
though I wouldn't object
to being one or more of those things
at some point in my life.
I mean, it would be nice to be
exposed to the elements
and to the eyes of a thousand passing truck drivers
and, in spite of it
or because of it,
remain standing.
To break down and
build up and
break down once more.
To accept the cycle, or
the challenge, or
the promise
of beginning again.
Hypothesis:
I am alive and so are you.

Kelly Frankenberg, an artist, writer, teacher, and comedian, illustrates and writes children's books, songs, poems, and screenplays. She wrote a memoir titled *Diary of a Gay, Pregnant Bride.* Her work has appeared on *Extreme Makeover: Home Edition*, Fox National News, Kare 11 News, and public television, in films and newspapers, and on windows, walls, pianos, and mailboxes.

Intent to Love

During my divorce, I found myself contemplating the promises we make when we get married. Can we love someone forever, or can we only *intend* to do that?

My mother had been divorced twice, widowed once, and left her fourth husband a widower. She always told me she never stopped loving my father, her third husband, who died from cancer, the love of her life.

My mother's best friend, Pam, my godmother, had married my mother's gay uncle, making her my great-aunt. To help me better understand love and marriage, I finally decided to ask Pam why she intentionally married a gay man. She invited me to her house to talk.

I stood on the concrete steps facing my great-aunt's glass door and rang the bell. Muffled barks of small dogs flooded the silence. I had arrived precisely on time to avoid criticism about my punctuality.

Pam, now in her sixties, loved to host and entertain. Years of practice made her a pro, and she took much pride in her talent. I compared her, at times, to Martha Stewart.

She opened the door, and three white Maltese dogs came running up to greet my shins. Prancer, the black and white cat, pressed his body against the back of the couch as he scaled it, running his tail gently along it.

The small Minneapolis house had the same décor I remembered from my eighties childhood, items that went back to the sixties or earlier. Everything was well preserved and ready to host guests. Generations of dogs and cats had lived on the furniture, though one could never tell. Light mint-colored velvet rugs welcomed feet, and rose-tinted wallpaper faded behind oval gold-framed paintings of old-fashioned women in nature.

But today, the house was transformed. It was nearing Christmas, so Pam's usual over-the-top themed décor transported you directly to December 25. I glanced around the living room. Snow villages resided on numerous counters. There wasn't one square inch that didn't have a sparkly or lit-up decoration. Even the tree tended to get lost beneath the thousand ornaments that nested on it, each one precisely placed. Rugs, napkin holders, napkins, towels, even paintings on the walls were switched out for ones with Christmas themes. Knickknacks, clocks, tablecloths, and, no exception: the treasured china in her china cabinet.

Pam collected dishes. Rare dishes, full sets of dishes. Punch glasses, ice cream dishes.

"Have a seat. Can I get you a cup of tea?" she asked.

"Yes, please," I said, setting my purse on the flower-patterned couch as two of the dogs parked their bodies next to me and on my purse.

Pam poured the tea from a white teapot with a pine tree on it, which matched the saucers.

Being a cat person, I leaned back on the couch, inviting my neck to be brushed against by Prancer, who jumped up on the back of the couch. He loved to sit on people's shoulders even though he was too large to fit on anyone's shoulders.

"Try the biscuits," Pam said as she sat in the lime-green chair I remembered that her mother had loved.

The lime-green chair used to reside in the corner. A memory of being scared surfaced. Pam's mother had lost her lower leg to diabetes. When I was three and four years old I was placed on her lap many times. For some reason I was convinced the fake leg was something scary that needed to be avoided, and sitting on her lap put me in close proximity to it. I remembered wanting to get down and away from it and the photo of me on Halloween, dressed like a witch, sitting on Pam's mother's lap with a frightened look.

I pushed the memory aside and went straight to the reason I came. "Why did you marry Jack if you knew he was gay?"

My aunt sighed. "Our . . . our marriage wasn't like that. Um, your Uncle Jack and I had loved each other from the time we first met." Pam stirred her tea with a teaspoon. "But Jack knew that due to his lifestyle it would be unfair of him to take matters further with me. We became best friends and spent many happy years traveling, eating out, and giving parties."

I pictured the room filled with people for her memorable, grandiose parties.

"Your uncle struggled with being gay and was even suicidal once. I had a feeling something was deeply wrong."

She took her tea bag out of her cup and set it on the saucer.

"And one night when I was visiting, he abruptly left and hopped on a bus. I was worried and I followed him in my car. That's how I knew he got on a bus."

I took a sip of tea from the fancy cup decorated with a poinsettia and petted the dog resting against my leg. Looking at my aunt, I noticed she wore the same style makeup from her youth. Her hand-colored senior photo on the wall, soft and faded, reminded me of Snow White: dark hair, fair skin, and red lips.

"I followed the bus to downtown Minneapolis. I kind of knew he would be all right if he was going downtown, so I went home."

"The funny thing is that many months later we had a conversation about the night he left for the bus stop. He said he was very depressed and just didn't want to be around friends. But he had seen my car and knew that I was following him all along. He said he found it amusing and somehow knowing I was there helped him put things into proper perspective."

The smallest Maltese scratched at Pam's pantleg. My aunt's voice changed to high-pitched baby talk.

"Are you hungry, Lucy?" She picked her up, holding Lucy under her arm like a purse. "She's my baby." She looked at the dog, who very much knew she was her baby. Then Pam continued.

"For many years after I first met Jack, he maintained a relationship with me that was totally devoid of his gay lifestyle. I believe he actually didn't want me to think he was gay so he tried to be as normal of a boyfriend as he could. I never acted as though I thought he was gay, since he obviously wanted our relationship to be the usual male-female relationship."

Pam got up and walked into the kitchen, still talking. The dogs jumped up and followed her. "One night we stopped at a friend's house for a drink. We were casually talking and out of nowhere Jack told me he was gay." She returned and gave each dog a brown, bone-shaped biscuit. "I told him I had always known. It was part of who he was and it was part of the reason I loved him, though in a platonic way."

One of the dogs whined for attention but stopped when Pam hushed her.

"This was the turning point in our relationship. We were the deepest of friends after he told me he was gay."

Pam's phone rang.

"It's probably Ken. I told him I'd take him to the store today."

I pictured Ken, one of Jack's friends, who had the mind of a fourteen-year-old in a fifty-five-year-old body. Gay, a heavy smoker, a wannabe rock star. Every few weeks he would send me and other friends a card in an envelope covered in stickers, seven stamps, and completely random song lyrics that had been in his head that week. The envelopes reeked of cigarette smoke and contained a CD copy of an album from the seventies and out-of-focus photos of his cat, a program on TV, candy bars, or a crowd of people at the Gay 90s bar. Nicest man you'd ever meet. Pam drove him places, and he helped her with her house and the dogs.

Pam went back to her story after the answering machine picked up the call.

"We spent the majority of our time together. I knew, of course, that he was pursuing his lifestyle. He was very private so he never wanted me to be around the gay community. Eventually, those barriers were removed and I met and was friendly with all of his gay friends." She looked around the room like she was remembering his friends in the house. "Ultimately, we did talk about marriage after we were much older."

"How long had you known him by then?" I asked.

"We had been friends for nineteen years."

The dog closest to me yawned. Still curious, I waited for her to continue.

"The biggest obstacle was my mother's need for my care. It would never have worked out for us to live together while my mother was still living with me."

A memory flash of the fake leg gave me a shiver. I cleared my throat at the silliness of childhood fears, most of which we don't carry with us to adult life; death being the one fear that never goes away. "Why did you think of marriage?" I asked.

"Because in every way but intercourse, Jack and I were committed to each other completely." Her tone shifted to more of a lecture. "There also is a time in your life when sex is not the most important thing. Affection, caring, understanding, and always being there for each other were important to us. We wanted to take the final step in commitment—marriage."

I reached for a biscuit.

"So, after my mother died, Jack kept me occupied because he knew I'd have a hard time dealing with her death. He redecorated Mom's room so I didn't have the constant reminder of her presence." She smiled with what looked like mixed emotions.

"He moved in and we started planning our Las Vegas wedding." She took a sip of her tea.

"You must understand that my family knew Jack for years and adored him. They knew he was gay and didn't hesitate to welcome him as a family member. My aunt liked him so much she helped make our wedding a family affair. All of her girls, their husbands, and their children attended the wedding. She and her husband hosted the wedding supper and supplied a case of champagne." She paused and cleared her throat. "It was . . . it was the happiest time in our lives."

"At the time, we had no idea he had AIDS."

I looked over at the wood-burning fireplace and saw their wedding photo on the mantle. It was true. She'd never looked happier.

I was ten years old when Jack died. All I remember was that he was dying. Other vague memories came back: his cheery disposition and the image of his cat, Merlin, lying on his chest. Pam had told many times the story of how Merlin got up on Jack's chest and lay there like the cat knew the moment of his death and was mourning or trying to keep his spirit from leaving.

"He wasn't sick when we married or anytime before it. Jack would *never* have married me if he knew. His biggest fear was that because of the ten-year age difference, he might have illnesses requiring me to care for him. Of course, at that time, we never thought that within two years he would be diagnosed. He often said, 'I don't want to be a burden to anybody.'"

I looked over to a shelf on the wall. It was the urn that held Merlin's ashes. Jack, however, was buried in a cemetery in Minneapolis.

My aunt reached to the small cherrywood end table and picked up a glass cat figure.

"Oddly enough, knowing he was dying made our love even deeper," she said, moving the figure in her palm. She stared at it for a moment. "And in the first days, after he knew and was still in the hospital, we had time to reflect on what we meant to each other. And," she paused, "to plan for the rest of his life, however long that would be."

Pam looked down at Lucy, but I could tell she wasn't looking at the dog. She said, "There came a night when something terrible happened regarding his illness and I had to give him more intimate care. I don't want to go into detail, but it was wrenching for both of us. It was so dreadful and I had to force myself to help him because it was pretty disgusting. I told myself I could do it because I loved him and nobody else could care more deeply about him."

She reached down and picked up Lucy and placed the dog on her lap. Pam still looked down at the floor like the memory was there.

"I took care to maintain his dignity throughout the ordeal and finally, when he was cleaned up and had new pajamas on, he fell into bed exhausted." She petted Lucy. "I felt pretty sorry for myself by this time. The whole ordeal had taken two and a half hours, but I decided to put that aside and said to him, 'That was hard on you, wasn't it?' He nodded and said, 'But I wouldn't want to go through this with anyone but you.'"

She finally looked at me. "If that isn't love between a husband and wife, I guess I don't know the meaning of the word."

A tear escaped from one eye. She pretended it wasn't there.

All three dogs flinched as I got up to hug her.

"Thanks for sharing your story," I said to her. "I wish I had known him longer."

"I have never given a moment's thought to finding someone else. After all, I had the best man there was and no one could ever compare to him. I miss him every day. I miss your mother, too."

"Me, too."

We stood in silence for a few moments. Then she said, "Well, I guess I had better go pick up Ken."

She and the dogs walked me out. Prancer lay on the lazy chair just as Merlin had laid on Jack's chest, with paws tucked underneath, keeping the warmth from escaping.

As I walked to my car, I couldn't help but wonder if we really get to choose who we love. Pam had experienced the one love for her lifetime. My mother, also. I could only hope to find that love—the love the heart is set on to love forever. And, perhaps, there is hope for others: those who have only an intent to love.

BEN FRENCH

Ben French is an interdisciplinary artist and writer originally from southwest Georgia. His play *tiny frightened animals* was the recipient of the Sam Selden Prize for Playwriting, the inaugural Bill Hallberg Award in Creative Writing, and the inaugural Young Playwright Award from the Dramatists Guild of America. His poems and artwork have also appeared in *Hello Mr.* and *Cellar Door.*

EMDR

after sam sax

RATIONAL(?)	IRRATIONAL(?)
you can think	
	like a wolf does
through anything	
	you can stick a probe
an android	
	into anyone's hand
slipping	
	like bloodied teeth
into the skin	
	& feel
of this world	
	nothing

its sheeple

so if

it's so easy &

you had a knife &

honestly just

never any remorse

getting away

with it

with anything

would you lie alone at night

when you're terrified

or rip open a boy who's caged

& already dying anyway

JULIE GARD

Julie Gard is a prose poet and educator whose publications include *Scrap: On Louise Nevelson*; *Home Studies,* which was a finalist for a Minnesota Book Award; and the chapbooks *Obscura: The Daguerreotype Series* and *Russia in 17 Objects*. She lives a block from Lake Superior with her partner, the poet Michelle Matthees.

Oil Change in Morehead, Kentucky

The men around us work on the car, hood lifted, while we sit inside listening to public radio. There is a child's drawing taped to the wall of the shop. The Supreme Court has just legalized gay marriage. We stare at each other and I laugh, say wow. We hold hands briefly between the seats. I didn't think it would happen in my lifetime, you say. We look out at blue sky through open wall. They check fluid levels and tire pressure. I can't believe this happened while we were here, I say. My grandmother grew up in these deep valleys that are like another country. A few miles and weeks away, a government clerk refuses to marry two men. At the folk art museum that afternoon, we pause in front of one man's fiery version of hell. Another man's heaven looks exactly like the valley we have come from.

Air Waves

Every once in a while I hear my ex-girlfriend's father on the radio. He is commenting on a potentially dangerous development in the American food supply, discussing the swift abatement actions of his branch of the federal government. My ex-girlfriend did not reuse plastic containers—BPA leaching—and she never ate bean sprouts—*E. coli*. She was careful of all sorts of things because of her father, who'd had a terrible temper when she was growing up. He was calm by the time I met him, with this reassuring voice that fills my car.

Ascent

—after Killarney Clary

Life is shaking the plush antlers of the flight attendant on Christmas Eve. Matter is my daughter's glasses, lost on the way to the airport. We grow always into the shape of our surroundings. There are our known environs, only those.

Tearing the cloud line, the sun breaks clear, blue sweater and white hair against it. The woman in front of me is faceless facing sky. We are delayed in Minneapolis due to fog in Philadelphia.

When there is too much space between Katharine Hepburn's life and mine, or when it is simply odd and disconcerting to sleep among the horses of the deep Main Line, I sit by a stream in a cleft of rock on one of the old estates. The empty fields we drive by on the way to my parents belonged to the heiress she played in the film.

I grew up part stranger, believing the myth of lost Jersey accents. To everything here is a worn shine. I stay up late in this place that I must be from, because there is nowhere else.

This Summer

Do you remember such green? The oiled feather and under—fresh mint. Sprigs of sorrel popped up. A roller coaster, flying bear, every last germination and riddled bug. Film on water, pocked stone, rooted plant, scrap of wing. What stays and what goes. We cannot mix or part. I do not know the curve and I fear your loss, so I wander the yard with my spade.

Standards season into refrigerator pickles. Garlic included along with feathers of dill. Snow gone and the cat's meow. I close the door against all but your hip. Eight minutes of warmth and a turn, a taste. The long-lasting jar here in bed. Eight minutes.

Aging wildflowers on the table. Just say touch, let new thoughts in. A bit of blue hair. How is her brother? May the day be ripe in places. Each picture a sign for another soft stop. My middle and stream. We fell into night and let day be day. How could she not be lonely? The paint is left around the house. So many books at once. Why is the heart in voluminous hair? In yours, mine.

In the blue room we float through the storm. Cats press to the floor. The dog's ashes stir. Old photographs follow the rain with their eyes. We float as it streams from soffits, the fireplace flue a bell. Your head against me is the only window open.

Twin Ports

The lake is not about words at all. It's only language if moans are language, and needs. It's only poetry if poetry's wet and shocking. The lake is what can't be said, what's never done, the work of the heart outsourced to this other body. As opaque as its ring of stones.

My friend searched for those agates that people love, stored them up and moved to the desert. I'm still here, stumbling and foraging the joint of the river, crossing it every day. Our students remember her. The lake is not about words at all.

Christina Glendenning, a writer and educator, has published two novels. *The Rattlesnake Vote* is a mystery whose main character, a homophobic detective, must rely on a transvestite prostitute to solve a murder. *Searching for Gods That Deserve Us* is a collection of related short stories.

To Love a Woman

There is a difference between making love with a woman and making love with a man. And this difference is not the obvious. Genital complementarity, the fit of male parts into female parts, is touted as the natural yin and yang of life. This "proof perfect" is what society ladles into our empty bowls so it can garnish the Sapphic love feast with shame and guilt. The truth is that physiology doesn't count for much at the end of the day . . . body pales in comparison to psyche. We women possess highly nuanced psyches. Our bodies, our very souls are layered with emotional and spiritual complexities.

As women who desire women, we weigh in on nuance, on the subtleties of emotions expressed and those pulsing below the surface. It is the ones that pulse that beg our special care. *Will you hurt me, will you listen to me . . . will you take the time to learn my body?* This is the soul-language of a woman searching for a lover. Very few men pulse this deeply below the surface. What is offered is three-dimensional intensity.

We women run deeper—there is a dance between dimensions. When attraction hits, you create openings offhandedly, safe spaces for her to test the waters. You decipher her woman's words and ponder the possible meanings as she looks into you and through you. You follow the breadcrumb trails of interest and intent; you cover your shyness with honey-soaked shrugs and small touches. A woman opens up worlds of anticipation and hunger. Worlds of need and temerity. She makes you weak; she makes you brave. Her body unmasks your desires; her vulnerability teaches you patience. By the time you connect, you are already inside her soul.

But this is about the quest for love, not sex by its lonesome. This is about the connective tissue between two souls and how it is forged first from simple proximity, then from touch and murmurs in the dark. No man has ever given you that, and you marvel at how you finally made your way to her.

Directness is traveling between two fixed points; this is true. But it's never a quick trip if it's to mean anything. And it has to mean something. Nothing between women can be truly measured in straight lines . . . we are always spinning in arcs of varying distance to and away from each other. We are lesbians; we were born to learn the dance of arcing toward the woman we want.

Then there is the sacred moment that you possess her. No touch is misplaced or inadequate. You know her body because you know your own. You no longer try for mutual orgasms . . . you want to watch her approach her release, then pull her back to need. You want to revel in what bodies do in their moment. You want to watch her face open to you wider than her arms around you—not be lost in your own desire.

But it's all about afterward, after you've had your fill of each other. Then come words as tactile as fingers. We cover each other with words like soft sheets that keep out the drafts of life. This is the soul at work, trying to create love, trying to create a home for itself.

Rachel Gold is the author of multiple award-winning queer and trans young adult novels, including *Being Emily,* the first young adult novel to tell the story of a trans girl from her perspective. Rachel is also a nonbinary lesbian, teacher, speaker, marketing consultant, all-around geek, and avid gamer. For more information visit rachelgold.com.

Kissing Kate Bornstein

"When are you going to get this chance again? Kiss her!" my friend Connie yelled across the restaurant.

In 1996, yelling encouragement for one girl to kiss another in a Sunday-morning crowded family restaurant in Duluth, Minnesota, was *not* the safest move.

But she wasn't talking about just any girl. Connie was yelling at me to kiss Kate Bornstein, which I really wanted to do.

The night before, Kate had performed at the University of Minnesota Duluth. She'd been touring her one-woman show after the success of *Gender Outlaw.* I was a baby dyke reporter with the local LGBT newspaper, covering the event but also hoping to hang out with Kate, especially after I saw her perform.

Her show began with the stage empty and Kate's voice over the sound system explaining how she'd learned to talk like a woman and then honed this skill by delivering phone sex. She even told us things she'd say to her clients, in her throaty, phone-sex voice. If you've never seen a Minnesota audience listen to a transgender woman doing phone sex—well, the frozen silence is deeper than any other you'll get in a northern winter.

Nobody moved. Some people stopped breathing. Minnesota audiences are already stoic, but now I could smell curiosity, arousal, terror. Over the next hour, Kate deconstructed the genders of a packed room of people like she was taking apart a set of Legos. She told her story while asking questions designed to make the most staunchly conservative Minnesotan question how they knew who they were. Most of them had probably never felt anything like it. I spread wings and soared.

Sunday morning brunch, I snagged the seat next to Kate and we chatted. That is, flirted. She was a lot better at that than me.

I asked if we could take pictures together for the newspaper, and my friend Connie got out her camera. Kate patted her lap. At twenty-five, I'd been out as a lesbian for almost a decade. I knew what to do when a girl like Kate invites you to sit in her lap—I did.

Is *girl* the right word? I think yes. Kate and I *were* being girls together. At points we were also women together and people and some other genders beside. This is what happens when nonbinary and genderfluid people hang out. I didn't have the language for it then, but in reading the revised edition of *Gender Outlaw* (2010—go read it!), I'm reminded that being human makes sense to me as a set of shifting, fluid roles meant to be played with.

Plus, hearing Kate tell her story of learning to speak and act like a woman felt very much like the way I'd learned to act like a woman. We came at it from different points—a nonbinary trans woman who'd been raised to act like a boy and an assigned-female person who had trouble understanding how to do binary gender—but the journey sounded remarkably similar in the middle. The way Kate talked about her experience was the way I felt mine.

This was a mixed blessing. After reading Kate's book and seeing her perform, I understood my experience better, but there wasn't a lot of language around it. We didn't have words like *nonbinary* and *assigned-female* in 1996, nor those ways of thinking about ourselves; I've included them here, anachronistically, because they're concise and powerful and I wish I'd had them. I had only the word *gender-queer*. I described myself as genderqueer on and off for years, but I felt the strongest kinship with trans women. In a sense there was a part of me saying, "I want to be a woman too," but not feeling like one.

This is supremely confusing when you look like a woman—or as some people unhelpfully put it, "could be so pretty if you tried." Confusing when you get treated like a woman and yet in many contexts being treated that way feels profoundly uncomfortable.

In my twenties, the only place I saw my experience reflected in any meaningful way was among my trans women friends. Kate walked through the world as a woman but also not a woman and not a man.

I vividly remember being at a conference with her—a few years after the "Kiss her!" moment—we walked to the restrooms and she paused outside those two clearly gendered doors and mused, "Hmm, what do I feel like today?"

At the same time, in the early-to-mid-nineties, my friend Debbie Davis still went to her day job in "drab" (dressed as a boy). She knew she was always a woman, but to the outside world sometimes she looked like a man. Much like my inside world, except mine contained a lot more than man/woman.

Back then in Minnesota if you were looking for transgender resources, you'd have found the Gender Education Center, which Debbie ran out of her home. Before the internet, and even after, it was one of the best resources for transgender women in the upper Midwest. As of 2014, Debbie had delivered 2,237 presentations to about fifty thousand people, "working toward understanding, acceptance and support for the transgender community." She's provided help for many workplace transitions, and she herself came out in 1998 in her job as a high school librarian.

Debbie and her partner Connie had driven up to Duluth with me. I'd fixed up the two of them on a date about a year before and it went fabulously, so Connie was trying to return the favor by encouraging me to kiss Kate. Debbie and Connie remained partners for years and were good friends to me as I struggled through a much less straightforward dating life.

A big challenge for me, growing up with the best trans women role models in the world, was that I never wanted to invalidate anyone's fixed gender. But how can I support your gender as fixed—that you're a woman and knew you were a woman even when everyone treated you like a guy—when mine isn't?

This is an ongoing conversation, but here's what I've got so far: isn't it possible, even likely, that some aspects of self are more fixed than others and this varies from person to person? I'm a writer and storyteller and will be at least until I die (and probably after). That's so much a part of me that without it, it would be very hard to be me.

The parts of you that remain constant might be: personality traits, like introversion; your love of family or animals or God; or maybe you're a quintessential teacher or engineer or clown. Most of us know a person with an unchanging aspect to them and other people for whom that was a phase or who move among aspects.

Why don't we treat gender that way? Why not simply accept that there are people who are women and are going to stay women, while there are other people who are sometimes women?

In most areas of life, we don't let the fact that some people change invalidate the fact that others don't. Why is this different for gender? Because gender as it's currently practiced is a system of power and oppression. (Many people have written deeply on that topic, so I won't go into it here.) Just because this system of gender tells us it's different from other aspects of being human doesn't mean that it is.

There are people who feel being a woman as a core aspect of their personality or soul and who are sometimes writers and sometimes painters, etc. And there are others who are always writers but only sometimes women.

But in 1996, I was still mostly a baby dyke, sitting in Kate Bornstein's lap with my friend Connie—a cis lesbian dating a trans lesbian—yelling at me to "Kiss her!" I looked at Kate and she grinned at me: a sweet, slow, flirty grin. I kissed her.

As I wrote in my journal at the time, "and then I guess we were making out in the middle of a family restaurant in Duluth."

Back then, I joked that if Kate was a gender outlaw, I should be considered a "gender in-law." In Kate's new edition of *Gender Outlaw*, this has come full circle. They (Kate now uses they/them pronouns) write, "transsexuals—those of us who saw ourselves as men and women in need of a physical transition—were gender outlaws. Today, trans men and trans women routinely tell me that they are not gender outlaws. And I agree. . . . If anything, they are gender in-laws, along with people who identify as cisgender."

Two decades after kissing Kate, I get to be a gender outlaw. And, since I wanted to be like Kate when I grew up, a trans feminine gender outlaw at that.

Molly Beth Griffin has authored two picture books (*Rhoda's Rock Hunt* and *Loon Baby*), a young adult novel (*Silhouette of a Sparrow*), a series of beginning readers, and two poetry chapbooks. She's received several grants and a McKnight Fellowship. She has an MFA in writing for children and young adults from Hamline University and is a teaching artist at the Loft.

The Exact One I Wanted

When I was eight months pregnant with my first baby, I ordered a glider from Babies R Us. The exact one I wanted. My partner cringed but she said *Fine, whatever, you're the one who will be nursing in it. Get what you want.* It was one of the few new things I bought for the baby.

I asked our friends to help me go pick it up, because our car was too small, because I shouldn't be lifting furniture, and they came. He and his wife came. So I was standing there, eight months pregnant, in Babies R Us, at the customer service counter, paying for the chair I'd nurse my baby in, with a man. And it suddenly occurred to me what people around us must think—that he was the father of my child.

And then it occurred to me that they were right. He was, technically, the father of my child.

But oh, this was not at all what they thought it was.

He was our donor. I was not his wife. His wife was waiting in the car, ready to help carry this giant box up the stairs of my duplex.

This whole arrangement was not what anyone in that store would guess. This whole arrangement was crazy. And perfect. The exact one I wanted. And I told them, in the car, what had gone through my head in that big box store of hetero-conformity, and we all laughed about it.

We'd been laughing about it from the beginning, actually. Because here is the truth: it is completely ridiculous to conceive a baby at home with a known donor. We asked them over dinner one evening, on our porch. We cooked. There was wine. It felt strangely like a proposal—will you do this thing, with us, this crazy thing that would tie us together for always? Actually I don't remember what we said or what they said, but I remember the giddy nervousness of the asking and the wave of relief at the response. Not only did they say yes, but they had already discussed it with each other and decided. They knew, or suspected, or maybe even hoped, that we'd ask.

It was exactly what they wanted, too.

Since nobody ever talks about these things, aside from *one* other queer couple we knew who had done it, we were basically on our own to hammer out the details. We drafted a document outlining expectations, trying to think of all the things we should agree to ahead of time. No, they wouldn't have any say in our medical decisions. Yes, any of us could move away from the others at any time. No, they would never fight for custody. Yes, they'd like to be involved in whatever way made sense.

And then, the trying began. And the ridiculousness escalated. I'd track my cycle meticulously; as soon as the pee stick gave the go-ahead, we'd find a time when he could come over. He'd show up; my partner and I would put a clean cup in the bathroom and go into the living room, purposefully ignoring the back half of the apartment. Then—quick swap! He'd come out, I'd grab the cup and the needleless syringe and head to the bedroom. In the beginning, my partner would come with me and we'd try to make it romantic. That wore off fast. It was better to just acknowledge that there was nothing romantic about this circus. It was better to let ourselves laugh about it.

It took us four months of trying, that first time. I knew that was not a long time, in the grand scheme of baby-making, but to me it felt like eons of riding the hope-and-disappointment roller coaster. We were all relieved when it took. The drama of conception quickly evolved into the drama of pregnancy, and The Purchasing of the Chair, and moments like it, when we were suddenly reminded that what we were doing was not *what people do*.

And at last we came to the drama of the thwarted home birth. After three days of labor and a hospital transfer and the birth of my ten-and-a-half-pound son, they brought us Chinese food. I ate it in my hospital gown, deep in trauma and exhaustion and also profound gratitude, as they took turns holding the baby we'd made together. It was ridiculous. And perfect. And exactly what I'd wanted, even though the birth was everything I'd feared.

A few years later we did it all again, with the added excitement of having a toddler in the mix. That took the circus to a whole new level of ridiculousness. And it took forever. I'd been regaled with stories of how fast second babies can be conceived, and I was ready for it to be quick and easy. It took a year and a half. Six months of trying several times per month, a break, and then six more months. We had it down to a numb routine by the end, and I was losing hope. I think everyone was. But it did finally take. And I was agonizingly sick for the entire pregnancy. I promised myself—and our donor—that after this baby, we'd be done. Our family would be complete, would be exactly what I wanted, and we'd stop this craziness.

My second birth was the absolute opposite experience from the first—a speeding freight train home birth and an eight-pound baby girl. Now, our family was complete. Not just because we had two children, but because we had this strange and complicated extended family to go with them. Over time we figured it out, calling our donors Uncle and Auntie, jumping through all the hoops of second-parent adoption, navigating the involvement of an extra set of grandparents added to our already colorful array of halves and steps.

It had been anything but easy, but we'd done it on our own terms.

As my kids grew up, the whole crazy arrangement became completely normal, for us. But not everything had turned out how we envisioned. My first baby became a child whose mind buzzed with a brilliance I never could have foreseen. He sorted lists of dinosaurs by era, and diet, and region. He made mazes adults could barely solve. He drew dragons breathing fire and wrote stories about them. His mind worked with precision that confounded me, and his teachers struggled to keep up.

But there was a dark side to all this. A perfectionism that haunted him. Aggression and rigidity that often stood between him and friendship. Senses so heightened that the sun was too bright, the traffic was too loud, the tastes and textures of food could be agony.

His little sister quickly learned how to push every single one of his buttons, and he responded by lashing out physically. Every day was a struggle.

We got special ed services in place and he began doing better at school, but at home, we walked on eggshells. I feared for my daughter's safety. He held her under the water at the wading pool in a fight over a floaty toy. He pushed her down our concrete front steps because he wanted to be first into the house. He grabbed a kitchen knife and threatened me once, I don't even remember why. I started getting more and more migraines, from the constant stress of policing their interactions. I stopped wanting to leave the house with them, for fear that the eruptions would happen at the park or in the grocery store. I no longer wanted to drive with both kids in the car, for fear that they'd fight and I'd drive off the road. Because one time I nearly did drive off the road, on the bridge over Lake Nokomis. I got us across the bridge, then pulled the car over and laid my head on the steering wheel while they clawed each other in the back seat. After that, I barely left the house. I dreaded the moment my partner left for work, and counted down the minutes till she came home. But not even the two of us could manage, not really. We needed help. Professional help.

But professional help, it turned out, can be hard to find. I had to cry on the phone to many, many people to get an appointment with a psychiatrist who would prescribe drugs to a six-year-old child. I wanted to explain, to the doctors, to everyone—we are hippies, we would never be doing this if we didn't absolutely have to. We are not people who jump to meds in a desire to have easily controlled kids. Those people, I was starting to believe, might be a myth. I suddenly had deep empathy for every parent I had ever judged for every decision I didn't understand.

Once our son was medicated, his aggression and impulsiveness eased up just enough that I felt like I could breathe. He was probably relieved, too. I cannot imagine what it would be like to be that out of control, that angry all the time. The meds slowed down his rage reaction, gave us a chance to calm him down before he hurt people. Gave him a better shot at friendship, and a real relationship with his sister. Allowed us all to enjoy each other, at least some of the time.

But I knew this struggle would always be part of our lives. We would always be asking how we could best care for this brilliant child, and also keep our whole family safe and healthy.

And for me, there was always the question, did I choose this? Because we knew autism was in our donor's family. They had told us about his brother's years of misdiagnoses that very first night, on our porch, over wine. We knew this was a possibility. And we built our family on these genes anyway. We chose a man who was smart and creative and kind. A man who was beautiful and generous and—yes—healthy. In himself.

But queer families have the burden of choice. We have to choose to get pregnant, and try diligently; there can be no accidents. We have to choose our genetic material; there can be no shrugging of shoulders, no *we work with what we have.* And so when something is imperfect, we wonder, could we have prevented this, had we chosen differently?

And there were certainly times, when my son was attacking his toddler sister for not knowing subtraction (we had to ban math at the dinner table), times when he lashed out at his only friend on a play date he'd been looking forward to for weeks, times when I made him a special dinner because he didn't like what the rest of us were eating and then he wouldn't eat that either, times when we forgot his sunglasses and he screamed and cried while I tried to maneuver through rush hour traffic—there were certainly times when I wanted to go back to that counter at Babies R Us and say, *no, no, this is not the exact one I wanted. I made a mistake.*

But of course I know that's not how it works, not for anyone. And even if we'd chosen a donor with a spotless family history, something would've cropped up. And then I wouldn't have gotten to raise this strange, beautiful boy, in this strange, beautiful family. This *chosen* family, built on trust and hope and friendship. This *chosen* family, built on laughter and a willingness to make it all up as we go along, because nobody handed us blueprints for any of this. I cannot regret this choice. Regret is not even an option here. Because love, I think, is bigger than perfection; it is the embracing of a whole, more complicated reality.

• • •

I used that chair till it was sagging and discolored. I nursed and rocked both babies in it. We moved it from duplex to house. Finally, I admitted that I needed something oversized and comfy to put in that corner of the living room instead, something I could curl up on to read with tall, bony children. I waited till I found the exact one I wanted, and ended up choosing something totally different from what I thought I was looking for—two red velvet antique chairs that could angle toward each other. No, of course they didn't fit in my car. But I had friends who were more than willing to help, so I bought them anyway. We carried them inside, together.

Now my partner and I sit in those red chairs to drink our coffee, while the kids rampage around us, driving us crazy. They are eight and four, and they're playing all these complicated pretend games together these days, with more stuffies than any two children should own. The games usually end with a fight and tattling. But I'm trying to see all the love in them too, the exuberance and the creativity. I'm trying not to expect perfection, or disaster either.

Because none of this is going to turn out exactly like I wanted. But the reality might actually be just fine.

CM HARRIS

CM Harris is the author of the novels *The Children of Mother Glory* and *Enter Oblivion*. Her short stories and essays have been featured in *O Magazine*, *Pseudopod*, *SALiT Magazine*, and *Harrington Literary Quarterly*. She lives in Minneapolis with her wife and their twins. She is also the lead singer of indie rock band Hothouse Weeds.

Defender

Yesterday Natalie had been Luke Skywalker; today she would be Han Solo.

When she awoke in the early dawn, it was from a dream of the *Millennium Falcon* landing on the front lawn, bending trees and torching leaves in its wake. But as the sun cleared the top of the fully intact cottonwoods, she realized it was off to Sunday church again in the new peach chiffon dress her aunt had sewn from a McCall's pattern. Now that same ruffled dress lay in a heap, a touch warm from her body (her "blossoming" body as Mom had recently begun stating) on the floor of her closet.

Natalie swaggered into Zoltar! Video Arcade & Movie Rental, her right hand hovering over an invisible, low-slung laser pistol. Save for the game consoles chirping and humming along the far wall, it was quiet in the arcade on a Sunday afternoon. No one stood at the front counter; it was just Natalie and the aliens, the asteroids and tanks. The wood paneling and carpet exuded its usual horse-poop smell of cigars and the remnants of spilt hair comb sanitizer. The arcade used to be a barbershop, but all the farmers sold off their land to developers and now everybody goes to Command Performance up north at the Oak Square Mall for layered haircuts.

Natalie strode over to the token machine. She fed a soft, five-dollar bill into the slot. It rolled back out mocking, like a pale green tongue. After a few more tries, the machine stopped kidding around and twenty gold coins hissed into the change cup. She strolled past *Defender* and *Tempest*, as if there were a choice to be made, and stopped at *Galaga*, her favorite game. Aliens rained down the scuffed monitor, begging to be blown into a spray of pixels. Her top score remained unchallenged. The player named REG was climbing, but NAT still crowned the list.

Natalie plugged in two tokens, smacked the start button, flicked the joystick, and let it *doink* back to center. Her right hand hovered over the fire button.

The stairwell door at the back of the arcade huffed open and a shadow crossed her periphery. She smelled the kid before she actually saw him. He was as aromatic as the boys who didn't bother to shower after PE. Even if Natalie were in the mood to ignore his funk and acknowledge him, she couldn't. The first wave of alien bees was sweeping down. If she didn't kill all of them during their entrance, she might as well say goodbye to a bonus—the whole game for that matter.

Natalie's right hand blurred and she fragged all the bugs before they had a chance to land in formation. The machine hummed low notes: *Ooom. Ooom. Ooom.* Her chest loosened its grip as she settled into her flow, the oncoming waves exploding with a satisfying rubber-ducky squeak: *weeko-weeko-weeko.* This could be an epic game, bonuses adding up. When Natalie was with the aliens her body was alert, focusing all energy into her eyes and hands. Time lost meaning. And the bugs kept coming.

Next to her, the boy stared into a *Tempest* game. The demo screen of spiderlike aliens climbed a vortex of webbed vectors. How long had he been there, just hulking around like a creep? Maybe he didn't have any money. Maybe he was soft in the head.

Eventually, Natalie looked up between levels twenty and twenty-one.

He smiled at her with big teeth, as if they knew each other. He had what was commonly referred to in junior high as the "bullshit mustache." Peach fuzz. It was dark against his pale skin. His eyes were a catlike hue, difficult to discern in this light, his hair a wet black. He looked like he didn't belong in this time period. Like the 1950s or something. What if he was one of those Chester Molester types? There would be no witnesses to her deflowering, or demise, or whatever he was planning.

Natalie jerked her stare back to the screen, began firing again.

"Hi," he said with a low, hoarse voice.

"Hey." She promised herself that if he came too close, she'd kick him in the knee.

"Can I watch?"

Heat filled Natalie's cheeks. "Free country." Or maybe she would punch him in the crotch and then sprint out the door, down the sidewalk, and over to the IGA, where Dad was loading up on this week's groceries.

He moved around behind her and landed in front of the game to her left.

"*Defender*'s better," he said.

She could afford to jerk a shoulder. "It's all right."

In *Defender*, the spaceship rocketed horizontally as opposed to *Galaga*'s vertical progression. In *Defender*, you piloted the ship up and down, backward, forward, exploring the stratosphere above a mountainous terrain. Having that much control, locked in profile, made Natalie uneasy.

The kid nodded. "*Way* more advanced. Feels like you're actually getting somewhere. And don't you love hyperspace? It's like you can feel it deep inside." He kicked the change box and the padlock rattled. "Got really good woofers in these things."

"Yeah." Natalie rolled eyes. Okay, she could easily take this kid. No witnesses.

"You're the first girl I've ever seen in here," he said. "You're really good."

Natalie kept tapping away at the fire button.

"I live upstairs," he said. "Stepdad owns the block."

"Must be nice."

"Not really."

He was silent for a while. She suspected she was supposed to ask why.

He sniffed. "I keep trying to get the high score but *some*body keeps beating me." She could hear the smile in his voice. "Want some cum gum?"

Natalie blinked. "Huh?"

"You know, the gum that cums in your mouth."

Natalie had heard Freshen-Up called that before. It was bubble gum with a gooey liquid center. It sounded dirty somehow.

"Why? Do I need it?"

The boy leaned in. "Want me to check?"

"No." Though she was adjusting to his odor.

"Here." The kid unwrapped the squishy cube and eased it into the side of her mouth. It felt like an invasion of body snatcher proportions, and the gum popped its goo before Natalie could get her tongue around it. She reached up to wipe her lip and botched the beginning of level twenty-four. Now the fire button was sticky.

"Um, great."

"Whoa, you're about to beat NAT. What's your high score?"

Natalie chomped away at the syrupy gum. "A mil."

"You *are* NAT."

She could not hide the grin. "Yeah." And forgot she had no more reserve fighters. An enemy drop-ship swooped down and snatched her last ship. GAME OVER. *Beedle. Beedle. Beedle.* A thousand points below her record. Sigh. Then Natalie botched the log-in. *NAG?* Gawd.

He extended a hand. "I'm Reggie."

She took it. It was soft, a little moist for her liking. "Okay, yeah, you're—" She wiped her hand on her jeans below the invisible laser pistol.

"Yeah, REG. Way down at the bottom." He chuckled. "So, what's your real name?"

"Nat."

Reggie looked her up and down. "You don't go to school here."

"No. In Hedburg."

"You're kinda cute," he said.

She cringed. "Okay."

"Wanna go on a walk?"

"Can't. Dad's picking me up. Soon." *Thank goodness. But not. I mean, maybe?*

The *Galaga* screen went blank before starting the demo. Just stars rising. Natalie's reflection stared back up at her. It was not the face it was supposed to be, not wry and clever. Instead, it was soft and desperate. Not even close to Han Solo. Too round. And the face next to it was the wrong face, too. He was no Princess Leia. If he grew his hair out, shaved his lip, and put on some deodorant, maybe.

And then she saw them. As if only his reflection could reveal it, like some sort of vampire situation. The breasts, his breasts, Reggie's breasts. Nat turned and glanced down at him, this time really paying attention. The boy had slight, conical breasts under his palm-trees-and-sunset T-shirt. He was no boy. Or he was. But he—

Natalie plugged more tokens into *Galaga* and started level one in rapid-fire mode, her throat closing off. She lost her first ship before level three.

"Man, your hand is fast," said this Reggie-person.

"Thanks." Natalie gritted her teeth. "Gotta keep a light touch." *Shut up!*

The thing was, Natalie's hands really were fast. And talented. There were many things those long, dexterous fingers got up to, not just video games, drawing, and guitar playing, or pulling laser pistols out of holsters, but what they got up to in bed at night. And in a Mr. Bubble bath. And sometimes in the garage, just because it was dangerous. No matter what would happen in her life, there would always be that skill, that pleasure at least. Maybe it was why she could keep up with the boys' high scores—the boys with their own fast hands. Someday her knuckles might be arthritic pearl onions like her grandmother's. But not today. Today they were weapons.

Natalie lost track of what she was fighting.

Reggie popped a bubble, blowing sweet breath at her, enraptured with the game or perhaps the reflection of their faces floating in space. Next to them, *Defender*'s stars striped into hyperspace. Warmth filled Natalie up to her neck. And it was there, right there in Zoltar! Video Arcade & Movie Rental, that she realized what cum gum meant.

Duh, you idjit.

Reggie leaned closer. "Your pupils are so dark I can see the game in them. Cool. Little explosions inside." He definitely had a personal space issue.

"Regina!" A man's voice thundered from the back stairwell. "Get your ass up here!"

"Crap." Reggie wheeled around and stared at the back door. This revealed a shadowy crescent circling the hollow between his right eye and temple, like a violent storm on a distant planet.

Natalie's hands trembled over the buttons. An alien dart hit her second ship and turned it into a roiling red cartoon cloud. She looked from the stairs to the storm on the kid's face.

His voice leapt into a soprano register. "I'll be right up!" He took her hand and shook it, the palm no longer moist. "It was nice to meet you, Nat."

The boards creaked in the stairwell, began to rumble, and then a tall, gaunt man pushed hard through the door and it slammed on the wall. His fury dipped below the surface when he saw Natalie. He murmured with a quivering lip, "I told you to get up—"

"Um, sir," Natalie said quickly, "Reggie was showing me how to play." She blindly jammed tokens into the machine.

The man's brow loosened and he chuckled, but he didn't sound very happy. "Girl, you don't want nothing to do with Regina."

"Well, I already put the money in. Just this one? I need help." Natalie gambled, "S-she's really good."

The man cocked a glance at Reggie and nodded. "Up in five." He opened the stairwell door and left with much less bluster.

"Thanks."

"No problem."

They played too fast through their rounds, both of them sloppy. The only thing keeping this kid from his awful stepdad was this dumb box of pixels, and here they stood, squandering their ships. Natalie gritted her teeth. What was the point? The kid had to go eventually.

On the last ship, Reggie peered out the front plate-glass windows, which were covered in a warped, tinted film except for a three-inch space along the frame. A station wagon had pulled up.

"That your dad?"

Natalie glanced up. "Yeah."

Reggie looked like a death row inmate in a made-for-TV movie.

"See you next Sunday?" Natalie asked.

The inmate brightened a bit, raised the corner of his mouth like a mercenary, and nodded slightly. "Next Sunday."

On the ride home, fat raindrops pelted the roof of the station wagon. Natalie turned off the air conditioning to enjoy the earthen, metallic scent. It grew stuffy.

Her father rolled down his window and opened a bag of pumpkin seeds, setting it on the vinyl between them. "Saw Tim from your class." He de-shelled a seed with his front teeth and flicked the wet husk out the window. "Did you know he bags groceries now?"

Natalie frowned; the shells were the best part. Salty. "Yeah."

"Asked about ya."

Natalie placed a bet on one of the raindrops racing up the dusty windshield. If it joined that one next to it, they'd be sure to make it. If it didn't, the wiper would sweep them away.

"His birthday's gonna be at the Great Skate on Saturday," he said. "Wanted to know if you got the invitation."

The odometer ticked off another mile. The two raindrops merged and spit off the windshield.

"I'm sure Mom will be fine with it." He cast a sideways glance at his daughter. "They got an arcade there, don't they?"

Natalie shrugged. It was a little late to be dangling the possibility of video games before her. *Galaga* was just a money sucker. And some boys were girls. And bravery came dressed in many forms. Maybe anything was possible.

Except a spaceship parked on the lawn.

That evening Natalie slunk off to her bedroom to sketch. She locked the door, hunched over her desk, and drew Han Solo with small breasts, bright feline eyes, and a bullshit mustache. Then she tore the sheet from the pad, signed it NAT, and hid it under her bed.

She lay there in the dark, unsure what to do with her fast hands, unsure what to even imagine anymore. Up on the bookshelf, her X-Wing and TIE fighter models stood poised in halted flight. In the middle of the room, a cardboard-backed photocopy of the Death Star hung from the ceiling fan by a strand of dental floss. It spun lazily in the breeze, intermittently revealing its lack of dimension.

ANDREA JENKINS

Andrea Jenkins is a poet, writer, and educator. She is currently the Ward 8 council member and vice president of the Minneapolis City Council. She holds an MFA in creative writing from Hamline University and teaches poetry at Minneapolis College of Art and Design.

Bag Lady Manifesto: (#sayhername/blacktranslivesmatter)

a deepened understanding of race and culture requires the
    following and then some more

        truth telling for immortality
recognition of historical trauma   an honest assessment of
    capitalism and its
        inherent violence

don't wall me in: Pilot said to the updated finger. They could
    perform all that jazz.

            carmen said Burning Blk Arts is
            a sin

WEDO what we do
      we do what they don't know
  we know what they don't know

blocks of art, talks, art, walks, art
dances on needles all scratchy like
a 78 wax recording of Bessie Smith.

lions' sleeping/ dreadlocked hair
with gray streaks of wisdom
quickened with the greens, the blues
oh yes the blues

am i blue?

hand over one eye, the good one
so eye can see you one more time
                    reFlection

Blk Bodies   Linking
                    All
      Oppressions
annihilating psycho-social development with lead-based drinking
    water

Cesaire—"Return to a Native Land"

the Blk queer literati are always classifying what we make as art!
always a quest for wholeness

                    I AM NARRATIVE

vernacular? always cool + coupled with the use of the body

let it play, BLACK

working against the forms given to us we make jazz, It's A Black Thang

This free Black Child of Transgender experience, of inner-city
Chicago, of stifling institutions of white supremacy, of great
shoulders to stand up on, of cristal dreams but andre's reality, of
"Hello from the other side," of curtis mayfield and the impressions

                              the body never forgets
                                        never
                                        never
                                        forget
                    this moment, ephemeral, "The
Beautiful Ones, they hurt you every time"

Oppression is the limitation of choices

Let us moan, so the devil don't know what we talkin' 'bout

ummmmmhummm ummm hummm mmmm hunmmm

Our existence is experiment, is created, is perpetuated, is sustained by individuals, but no less a system

looking back once upon a time, i sat on panels upon panels and nobody was selected from the first round or the second round, she wore a winged pendant on a tarnished silver chain that left a green ring just over her neckline, but she wasn't selected either

is this a witches' brew, she asked when it was time to leave, red beans and brown rice were being served to the late home comers, the catfish was burnt and the chicken wings weren't done yet, there is an equational relationship occurring under the surface

it is not really a rule that Black men shouldn't date doe-eyed, big-booty white girls, but the consequences are significant enough to make him think otherwise, other times . . .

there was an artist that fell to earth and shook the ground
let's dance they said, under the serious moonlight, the serious moonlight

rainbows and roses, pink cashmere coats, diamonds and pearls are a few of my favorite things.

sleeping lions dream of a day filled with naked juices and juicy fruits, all of a sudden there are angry protesters demanding justice

BLACK LIVES MATTER
they shout from the rafters above the fray, but the feels are real
   though
Black Brilliance=Miles=Billie-Malcolm=Harriet=Sacred Spirits

Ten Seventeen Twenty Fifteen
Bearing Witness at Fire and Ink
we represent, submerge, consider, make, survive, archive, document,

the essence of passages, of journeys, the soul's genesis is identity
existence surges, rhymes, sparks, transitions, a treasure is Art that
speaks of hope and love.

I heard there's a new Black Panther emerging, that dude that makes
the case for reparations, but i wonder is he thinking about gender-
neutral bathrooms? for his mama, and grandmama, and his son's
baby mama. You don't have to be a woman to be a feminist you
know.

i go to political rallies at malls in america, halls of capitalistic greed,
and i struggle, forced to move between two sides

Black   Trans

1 for the love of power
1 for the sake of power
1 in service to power

that becomes my relationship to risk, connected strings of images
that bring you to a moment—to connect your experience to what is
happening onstage

everything you do
everything you don't do
Deceives

When I love, you are no longer my enemy
But the words you spoke I keep within me.

Langston Hughes once said "nobody loves a genius child"
My Beautiful genius children stay getting murdered in the streets

Black Trans girl brilliance, shining too too bright
The boys on the block can't escape their light

They reach to the heavens, but the girls throw shade
They step back to their villas, to sip Lemonade

The recent increase in celebrity "visibility" that clearly
Does nothing for the most vulnerable

Makes us all targets for bigots in statehouses
Whose hatred is uncontrollable

Black women carry around pain in brown paper sacks, in shack
packs, in Louis Vuittons, Chanel, and Coach, sometimes it's a
laundry bag that looks too heavy
Or a backpack, or a diaper bag, "damn Ma what you got in yo' purse,
    a .45?"

We carry the weight of movements strapped over our shoulders,
    burlap sacks filled with dead bodies

#sayhername

Monica Loera—43 y/o Trans woman
Jasmine Sierra—52 y/o Trans woman
Demarkis Stansberry—30 y/o Black Trans man
Kayden Clarke—24 y/o Trans man
Nadine Stransen—89 y/o Trans woman
Kedarie/Kandicee-Johnson—16 y/o Black genderfluid person
Kourtney Yochum—32 y/o Trans woman of color
Maya Young—25 y/o Black Trans woman
Veronica Banks Cano—Trans woman of color
Shante Thompson—34 y/o Trans woman of color
Keyonna Blakeney—22 y/o Trans woman of color
Reese Walker—32 y/o Trans woman of color
Mercedes Successful—32 y/o Trans woman of color

T. T. Saffore—20-something Trans woman of color
Crystal Edmonds—32 y/o Black Trans woman
Rae'lynn Thomas—28 y/o Black Trans woman
Erykah Tijerina—36 y/o Trans woman of color
Skye Mockabee—26 y/o Black Trans woman
Dee Whigham—25 y/o Black Trans woman
Deeniquia Dodds—22 y/o Black Trans woman
Goddess Diamond—20 y/o Black Trans woman
Amos Bide—36 y/o Trans man of color
The Human Touch

Strategize tomorrow, but when we say tomorrow, we really mean
        today.

Today breathe sigh shed tears

laugh

if that helps.

Call your mama
            brother
            daughter
            sister
            son
Tell them/you love them
Tell them we survived terrorism before
Lived through dehumanization and cultural starvation

Tell them not to think about
unarmed black folks
assaulted
killed—
for holding guns
selling loose cigarettes
listening to rap music at a gas station

for knocking on the door and asking for help
for wearing bikinis at a pool party
for laughing on a wine train
for wearing hoodies
for going to church

Tell them to strategize about that tomorrow, but when we say tomorrow we really mean today.

KRISTIN JOHNSON

Kristin Johnson lives in Minneapolis with her wife, her stepson, and their two Labradors. She has won two Minnesota State Arts Board grants and published nine books for children, including *The Endurance Expedition, The Orphan Trains,* and three books in Lerner Publishing's "Day of Disaster" series.

A Thousand Reasons Why

Because of the time you said,
I hate that word. Do you even *know* what that means?
When I didn't answer, you said,
I hope none of *my* kids are.

Or the time we went to *Brokeback Mountain* and you said,
I thought it was just going to be a western!
And I didn't know what to say.
And then you said, I know those things go on, but I don't want to
    see it!
And I said it was a work of art.
And then you just made that *hmmmm* noise.

So that's why.

Bridges and Branches

"Is there anything you want to tell me?" Dad asked.

The question hung between us like a bridge swaying gently side to side but missing too many of its floorboards. His directness surprised me. I clung to the frayed rope railings and searched for something to say, but I ended up focusing on the oxygen tubes dangling from Dad's nose.

It would be foolish to tell him now, wouldn't it? He'd have a heart attack. The tubes branched out toward tanks in the corner.

"No," I said, shifting in my chair.
I glanced at him, then changed the subject. I was good at that.

I picked up a poem I had typed and brought with a handful of others: Joyce Kilmer, one of Dad's favorites. Dad always thought he was funny when he would ask me, "What was the most famous poem *she* wrote?" Dad made this joke many times; he would laugh so hard. "Because Joyce Kilmer was a man. You get it?"

Yeah, I got it.

That day, I recited Kilmer's poem to Dad, but for some reason I choked on the last two lines:
"Poems are made by fools like me / But only God can make a tree."

Dad died a few days later. I was pretty sure he already knew. Yeah, he knew.

● **BRONSON LEMER**

Bronson Lemer is the author of *The Last Deployment: How a Gay, Hammer-Swinging Twentysomething Survived a Year in Iraq*. His work has appeared in *Blue Earth Review*, the *Reykjavik Grapevine*, and *Twentysomething Essays by Twentysomething Writers*. He lives in St. Paul.

Chameleon Boy

Between the wooden slats of the bookshelf in my living room, I see Donald Trump on the back cover of a comic book. He is crouched in the lower corner, an intruder poised at the edge of my life. I first noticed him a few nights ago—creeping, watching—and now I imagine him lurking in other places around my house. I imagine him in the bathroom, his scowling face peeking out from inside the tub. Behind the toaster, in the onion patch, tucked inside my sock drawer. I imagine him smirking while watching me sleep.

I tell this to my boyfriend, Matt. It is his bookshelf, his book.

"This guy?" he says, pointing at the Trump look-alike. "He's not even human."

It doesn't matter whether the figure is human or not. I know the figure isn't *supposed* to look like Trump, but that is what I see, and what matters to me now is that Matt sees Trump too.

I've been thinking a lot about permanence lately, how moving things become still, remain, shift into something else. This bookshelf is in my first house—my first real home after years of moving around—and Matt is the first boyfriend I've ever asked to move in with me. It feels very concrete, very settled. But also very raw, all the jagged edges of our new relationship rough and ready to harm. I worry that he won't like it here, that I won't like *him* here. I worry that he'll get bored. I worry about change—him changing me, me changing him, neither of us changing at all. Mostly, I worry about not seeing eye to eye.

"Chameleon Boy," Matt says about the Trump look-alike. "From the Legion of Super-Heroes."

I know nothing about Chameleon Boy, so when he says this, I imagine a half-lizard, half-boy creature with the ability to morph into just about anything—a bird, a rocket, a billionaire with an unnatural-looking comb-over. I imagine a superhero constantly changing, never still, someone who easily blends into his surroundings. I picture a character similar to X-Men's Nightcrawler, a creature I emulated in my twenties with my constant moving, my nonstop wanderlust. Job to job. Place to place. Boyfriend to boyfriend. I never stayed with anything for longer than two years. I morphed, changed, moved on when the camouflage wore off, when I realized I would probably never really fit in.

"Yeah, but doesn't he look like Trump to you?" I ask. "Don't you see it?"

I think about those ambiguous images I saw when I was a child, the ones where some people see one thing and others see something else. Once, our teacher showed us a black-and-white figure and asked us what we saw. My classmates said they saw a young woman. I stared at the figure until I saw the woman too—her feathered hat and billowy veil and furry coat. Then, our teacher asked, *Do you see the old woman?* I squinted hard at the figure. All I saw was the young woman, her single eyelash and small nose turned away. I tried to see an old woman in the figure, but I couldn't make my eyes see what I wanted them to see. Instead of raising my hand and asking the teacher to point it out, I pretended I saw the old woman because my classmates said they saw her and I didn't want to be left out.

Now, I want Matt to see Trump on the comic book so I can know that our relationship will work out, that I've made the right choice in asking him to live with me, that I belong in this house with him. But Matt doesn't see what I see. He sees Chameleon Boy and only Chameleon Boy, and instead of thinking our relationship is doomed and that I should run away like I've always done before, I just smile back at him and try to imagine the hazy space between being one thing and being something else—that middle ground where everything seems to float or flutter or vibrate because it doesn't know which direction it should go. *Is it a young woman looking away? A shape-shifting alien? Or is it something else, something blurry and obscure, something difficult to define and pin down, something never still?*

Later, I'll ask Matt questions about the characters in the comic books he reads in bed—Animal Man, Ragman, the Creeper; so many men pretending to be something else—and we'll argue about the meaning of the term *secret identity*. He'll say that it refers to a super-hero's civilian identity, when they aren't assuming their superhero persona, and I'll disagree. I'll argue that they are civilians *first*. Then they become something more, take on alter egos, shift into other identities. The superhero identities *are* the secret identities, hidden from others, not the other way around.

Matt will laugh, shake his head. He wouldn't hesitate to tell me I'm wrong.

RAYMOND LUCZAK

Raymond Luczak is the author and editor of more than twenty books. His latest titles include *Flannelwood*, *A Babble of Objects*, and *Lovejets: Queer Male Poets on 200 Years of Walt Whitman*. He lives in Minneapolis.

Molly

In the mine shaft anything can happen in the dark far below. It isn't the kind of hell that the church folks like to describe, but its trapdoor opens quickly if you're not careful.

A cart, so heavy with raw ore, can topple and jam the rails and knock one of the support beams asunder.

Anything can happen, including death.

These men know full well what they are getting into, especially those who've crossed the Atlantic Ocean to arrive here.

I don't know their languages but I want to ask again and again when I read the headlines about the latest mining accident: is it still worth the long hours for such low pay?

But I never ask.

Everyone knows me as Anna Marie Bergman, but they call me Molly.

They also say I'm a very good cook.

I have golden flax hair.

I have freckles that disappear whenever I blush. But I don't blush anymore.

People think I'm originally from Sweden, but I grew up in America. My parents made a point of conceiving me a few months before they stayed in steerage across the Atlantic. They wanted to make sure that their first child would be born American. They'd heard all sorts of talk about how the American government was looking for ways to reduce the number of immigrants jamming Ellis Island. What was clear at the time was that immigrants with children born in America wouldn't be deported.

I knew nothing of my parents plotting so deviously until years later.

All I learned growing up was that it was hard for my parents trying to eke out a living in Stevens Point, Wisconsin. They'd known a few good friends who immigrated there. Times had been difficult in Malmö, but they hadn't realized how much harder America would be.

Nevertheless, they chose to stay for the next twelve years in Stevens Point.

Where else could they go? They'd gambled away everything but the clothes on their backs and a few precious heirlooms in their one trunk.

Then my father learned of Ironwood, Michigan. Mining jobs on the Iron Range were very easy to get.

He moved all of us up here.

We made do in a drafty house in the Ashland Location. We didn't know how brutal the winters were to come. But then again winter was part of our Swedish blood so it was not a concern.

I sorely missed my friends in Stevens Point.

My father died four months into his new job in Ironwood. The powder of iron had taken possession of his lungs until he couldn't cough anymore.

The look of his eyes, freshly dead, is something I will never forget.

Two days later Ma found a new job. I had to quit school and work as a maid at Solomon Curry's house. My younger sister Jenny had to work too.

My body began to age quickly.

I wanted to fall asleep when I scrubbed the ballroom floor, but the clamor of feet in the hallways everywhere was the sound of an army marching forward to the tune of a shiny copper penny hitting the bottom of a piggy bank. I felt as if all of us maids, servants, and cooks were on a ship, constantly rowing with no land in sight. Sunny days felt like cloudy years.

This was how I'd spent my days while thinking of my daughter. My Ingrid.

Two days ago you, my husband, died. One of the beams holding up the underground tunnel collapsed. The weight of earth and ore crushed you and three other men.

People wrote again about the need for stronger safety measures.

The talk of setting up a new labor union drifted around town, but most of the workers didn't speak English. No unity. They were afraid of losing their jobs and being deported.

The women in Mr. Curry's employ do not question why I'm not filled with melancholy over your passing. They seem to understand, as I do, that sometimes the men we have in our lives aren't necessarily the ones we want.

Some people called Mr. Curry "Mr. Ironwood." He kept me around after Ingrid was born. I have caught the flicker of desire in his eyes. His wife had died some years before, but with Mr. Ironwood, nothing inappropriate ever happened. After all he was in his seventies. He had started up two new banks and laid out the streets of the fledgling city twenty years ago. He ran the Metropolitan Iron and Land Company until he lost control of it in the Panic of 1896. He served in the state legislature for a while. He tipped us well. But he was nothing like those men just striding into the room of our lives and closing all the doors except one where we become indentured to the grindstone of raising their children. They like the idea of making sons and naming them after themselves. They don't want the toil of looking after them. Babies are tiresome.

You are dead.

The tension in my shoulders is gone.

Ma doesn't say anything about you; she doesn't need to.

She had seen the fierce repugnance in my eyes whenever you appeared.

I didn't want to marry you, but I had to.

You forced your way into my most private room.

When I saw I had no blood the following month, I asked Ma why. She wept.

I didn't understand why at the time.

But you and I had to marry right away at the Swedish Lutheran church. Nothing fancy. We had no money for a wedding reception.

There was no love in your eyes when you bedded me that night.

I had no desire for you.

I didn't know that pain could have many new names.

But I didn't experience any pain during the funeral service in your name. They all thought I was being stoic. After all, Swedes weren't supposed to be emotional.

Now that you are gone, buried so easily at no cost, I am glad that I didn't have to foot the bill for your coffin.

My mother didn't press me when I said I had no money for a tombstone.

No one offered to help pay. We were all too poor.

I think we had become infected with the virus of the American Dream. As long as we stay put in this country, death remains the only cure. Each mine shaft collapse becomes a cemetery. The great shovel of God leaves behind gaps of the raked earth. Sometimes the miners slide piles of soil into the pit, flattening as well as they can. They dismantle the headframe and erect brick fences to keep out the onlookers. Then it's time to build a new mine shaft.

Sometimes the ones who own the mining companies will demand to make the mine shaft bigger. Fix the broken beams. Dig out the grisly corpses for two extra dollars. The demand for profit is stronger than the waft of death rising from the seemingly endless well of ore.

Sometimes when I walk along Suffolk and look south, I see my father's ghost waft upward now and then.

He doesn't say a word to me.

I know how truly sorry he is.

I've long forgiven him.

What I cannot forgive is how you chose to treat me the way you had.

I hadn't realized how easy it was to delude myself. I thought that being your wife, I'd have more respect from you.

The looks of those who knew me well told a different story. They all knew why we'd married, but they never lent a word of understanding.

But you are dead.

Why must I mourn you when you'd spent more time with these men whose names I barely know than with me? I was good enough for a lonely hour or two. No one had ever instructed me how babies could be made.

You simply flirted with me. I had no prior experience with men. I'd sensed that I should say no, but I hadn't thought that highly of myself.

You left your seed inside me, and I bloomed with a flower in my arms.

Your last name attached to mine is a bloodstain that never dissolves after repeated washings. Ingrid will learn her father's name, but I will never tell her stories about you. I will not mythologize a man who cared only about the bone between his legs.

Sometimes you forgot my name and confused me with a few other girls you'd known. Their names, uttered out loud in your awful grunts, were like ice picks in my heart.

Sometimes you squandered your week's pay in the sleazy bars that lined Silver Street on the other side of the river.

I didn't have the heart to tell Ma what happened, but once she found out, she didn't hesitate to lash out at you.

I'd never seen you look so cowed.

I wanted to applaud when you came straight home with all of your pay the following week.

My arms and fingers were always sore when I came home from Mr. Curry's house, so I asked you to hold our daughter for a while. She was having a colicky fit.

You didn't want to rock Ingrid and pat her back until she calmed down.

I wanted to cry. How could you be so cruel?

Ma shook her head and stopped kneading the dough for rye bread. "*Jag trodde du var en riktig karl,*" she spat out as she wiped her hands on her apron and took Ingrid from my arms.

You left.

That was the last time I saw you.

The following morning you must've been slightly drunk and come to work anyway, or you hadn't slept all night. We will never know.

Either way you stumbled your way in the dark below.

For that I'm glad. I'm just so sorry that others had to die with you. They didn't deserve to.

I've met with their wives and children a number of times. They're still learning English, but they're my friends now.

They rarely talk about the husbands they've lost.

I don't ask questions.

They don't ask me either.

Our faces are focused on the flickering flames of our future.

Sometimes we take turns looking after each other's kids. They give us sparks of joy.

Why must I mourn you when you'd spent more time with buddies whose names I barely know than with me?

You used to say I was too smart for my own good.

Men like to remind me how no one likes me. I'm not ladylike enough.

So I have to pretend.

I set aside a few pennies every month to send to the National Woman's Party. The papers keep attacking Alice Paul's suffrage crusade, but she is my idol. The Silent Sentinels are my heroes, marching six times a week in front of the White House while Kaiser Wilson hobnobs with powerful men who don't want us around when they smoke their expensive cigars. I hope to be as strong as them.

I never tell anyone my dreams. Who would understand?

All I want is to have my Ingrid grow up differently than I have.

One day women like us will be able to walk into the voting booth and press the lever the same as any man. We will not be denied ever again.

One day my vote will matter. It will force ugly men like you to stay out of our lives.

The First Musk

The warm air, thick
with misted humidity,
hung low around us
one February morning.
I dawdled behind
my deaf classmates,
ski hats and mittens
stashed into our jackets
left unzipped
in the hot steam
of the crisp sun
magnified through
the glass high above us
where the crystal lace
of ice and snow
graced the edges
of each pane.
Facing the seven of us
(including a teacher
and her aide)
crowding the aisles
between tables
loaded with plants
of all kinds and sizes
in green plastic pots
labeled with numbers
stood a tall woman
who smiled a lot,
who wore long, frizzy hair,
who wore jeans
with wet knee stains.
I was surprised
this hadn't bothered her.
Mom always used

a dark lime-green
polyurethane kneepad
on the kitchen floor
when she washed it
clean of footprints
every Friday afternoon.
Why couldn't this woman
do the same thing?
Standing before us,
she explained
slowly and carefully,
as if she was afraid
to shout at us,
forbidden to sign
and too young then
to question such fallacy,
how a plant could grow
from a seed
*Look at how small
this is* into *This!*:
a tall plant in a huge pot.
It didn't look
like anything familiar,
not from the summers
I'd spent across the street
from my house
in the woods
where breezes sifted
dandelion whiskers
flurrying through
the saplings
crowding against
each other, spectators
lining the motorcycle trails

us kids raced on foot
in search of
another adventure.
Foxes and rabbits
startled us
with their tails,
tipped with white,
hopping back
into the basket
of tall grasses
that itched our faces
when we plowed
forward north,
off the trails,
where the cave-ins,
remnants of iron mines,
steel shafts
long dismantled,
already blanketed
with the grass of time
sloping down
to a circus of saplings.
Down there we explored,
darting around the slender
trees, not knowing that
a few summers from then
a bulge of water would
push up from nowhere,
filling the big holes
and drowning the saplings.
Melted snow would add
to its unmarked depths.
Every winter since
we would be told *Never
go down there!
Too dangerous.
There's no telling how*

thin that ice is.
In the greenhouse
we deaf kids stood,
looking agape
when the woman pushed
her long fingers
right into the soil
near the plant's stem
and burrowed
deeper, deeper
Wait I got it
and twisted
her hand just so
until she pulled out
a tiny brown ball,
the smallest potato
I had ever seen.
Every winter
in the evening
my father plotted
on scrap paper
our two gardens
in our backyards
(he'd owned two houses,
ours and the one next door
that he rented out,
and a third lot
for our three-car garage),
poring through
Burpee Seeds catalogs
while the nine of us kids
ran around the house,
all cooped up
while he awaited
the prison of winter
to release all of us
in the freedom of summer.

He rotated the crops
between our two gardens
so the rows every year
were never the same.
He made us siblings
march up and down
the foot trails so
they wouldn't feel mushy
between the ridges
where he'd planted
one seed after another
and anointed each seed
with a pour of water.
We had to stamp hard
until we felt hardness,
a sense of something
like crooked concrete.
Then the rains came.
The seeds sprouted.
One row had fuzzy
carrot tops that drooped.
Another row exploded
in upturned lettuce wigs.
A short row shrouded
budding watermelons
in huge talon leaves,
nestled in springy tendrils.
Two rows lined crooked
daggers until they turned
into swords of corn.
The sugar snap peas
were my favorite snack.
I stole a few pods
whenever I was hungry.
Mom always complained
there were never enough.
She gave us kids dirty looks.

Mornings each of us took
turns to pluck out weeds,
those errant fingers
peeking out of the soil.
Done, we came running
back into the house,
its side door banging
behind us, shouting, *Mom,
I did two rows,
Can I go play now?*
Our fingernails
showed gray crescents
so we enjoyed
clipping our nails
over the opened toilet
where we brushed
away the tiny soil wedges
and made our nails clean.
That was always fun.
The soil we packed
in our two gardens
was only the color
of light brown sugar.
No distinct smell to it.
In the greenhouse
I couldn't stop
staring at the soil's dark
chocolate color.
How could it look so *black*?
The dirt across the street
where mottles of birches
and tall grasses swayed
revealed a rust color,
a nod to the old days
when miners from Croatia,
Finland, Ireland
Germany, and Poland

slid down into
the gaping shafts,
gods in full mastery
of house-sized machines,
and carved out
huge chunks of iron ore
that would soon be
hauled away by train.
Such glory days
were long gone
by the time I was born.
I didn't understand
how these immigrant men,
inured to long hours
in the pits of earth,
were already longing
for something real, perhaps
a song from their childhoods
back in the Old World
that would root them firmly
home here in America.
In the greenhouse
I looked up at the woman.
I don't recall what I asked,
but she answered,
her eyes alight,
handing me the baby potato,
more like a marble
really, the kind
the hearing boys and I
won on the ground
outside Ripley School
where we twisted
the heel edges of our tenners,
into the hard dirt until
the hole was big enough
to accommodate

the many scores
of marbles we flicked
with our thumbs
as far as we could
during recess each fall.
We traded marbles
every single day.
It meant we were *boys*,
a world of our own.
I didn't quite understand
how the hearing world worked,
but I knew it involved
strong and nimble thumbs.
I didn't know it then
but those days
when I finally felt a part
of the world around me
were coming to a close.
Soon the marbles
would disappear
into our pockets,
as if they'd become
objects of shame,
and give way
to standing around
nonchalantly
by the vacant marble holes,
making lots of talk
about the TV shows
we'd seen the night
before, sometimes
reenacting them
but nothing like how
all of us had moved
in slow motion,
wanting to be the next
six-million-dollar man.

We would all be Steve Austin.
Their mouths now moved
quickly with new words
I'd never lipread before,
and I wanted to know
when we could play marbles
again. I felt a slight rage
rise, just like how Jack
had grown his magic beanstalk,
from the handful
of marbles I'd caressed
in the secrecy of my pocket.
I'd worked so hard
to win each single one,
some truly beautiful;
I even practiced
secretly after school!
And all for what?
I didn't grasp yet
the stir of hormones
lurking beneath
our skins, waiting to shed
the smoothness
for a coat of peach fur,
or that in a few years
our voices would crack
into a deeper register.
Without warning
they turned to me.
I was that waif-boy
with those things
in his ears. Nope,
I wasn't one of them.
On the bus home
that afternoon, I sat
near the front,
no longer cool enough

to sit near the hearing boys
in the back seats,
and felt the coolness
of my marbles
clinking softly
between my fingers
as I watched the boys
jab each other
in the armpit
and break into guffaws
in the panoramic mirror
hovering above
the driver's bald pate.
The next morning
I saw how they moved
off to the side. I joined
my deaf classmates.
It was the first time
I came to understand
deaf kids weren't cool.
In the greenhouse
I weighed the baby potato
like a marble. So light,
unimaginably so.
They weren't the potatoes
my mother peeled
every Sunday noon
before boiling them
for mashing. I looked
at the baby potato
cradled in my hand.
Its dark residue of soil
had been wiped away.
I looked up at her.
She probably asked,
What's wrong?
I walked over to the big pot

and touched the soil.
It was loose. Soft.
Not densely packed.
I scooped a little bit.
Inhaling it, I felt a shock.
The smell on my fingers
was sublime, unlike anything
I'd experienced. Primal,
it sang of something
deeper than the earth itself,
its purest essence.
It flashed me back
to lazy July afternoons
where I spread
a rug on the grass
under a canopy of shade
and fell asleep
while cracks of sun
crisscrossed my face.
Awakening an hour later
was my favorite part.
My head woozy,
full of dreams elsewhere,
I always forgot
where I was
for a moment
as the sun lapped my face
like a happy dog.
I wanted to believe
I was transported
to another world.

What country would I find
if I didn't recall
which way was home?
In the greenhouse,
staring at my fingers,
I didn't know soil
could smell like *that*,
so rich and heavenly.
It was the first musk
that made sense to me,
my first flowering
into the world of men,
secreted by pheromones,
soon to be sprayed
with the cologne of desire.
I wanted to rub my face
across my hands.
Suddenly I didn't
need marbles anymore.
These days
I roast baby potatoes
until perfectly marbled
from a thin patina
of olive oil
in a cast-iron skillet.
Eating these
brings me back
to the boy
who nearly became
a man too soon.

Catherine Lundoff is an award-winning writer, editor, and publisher from Minneapolis. Her stories and articles have appeared in such venues as *Callisto: A Queer Fiction Journal* and *Nightmare Magazine*. Her books include *Silver Moon, Out of This World: Queer Speculative Fiction Stories,* and *Scourge of the Seas of Time (and Space)*. Her website is catherinelundoff.net.

Strange, But Not a Stranger

Feral: the act of escaping into or going back to the wild. Of leaving behind the promised security of a bed, shelter, and regular meals, of choosing outside over inside. Sometimes you choose to be outside; other times it chooses you. On the one side, you can see the camps lit by campfires, kept alive and warm by belief, by genuine connection, by semi-rhetorical devices like "sisterhood." On the other side are the walled villages and enclaves of church and state-sanctioned ceremony and stability.

I have found myself roaming between the two, vacillating between hungry and lonely, wild and tame at different times in my life. I was straight, in my own way, all through high school and college. It didn't always sit well with me, but—always more of a doer than a thinker—I didn't dwell on it. I had a string of boyfriends and a lot of booze to numb me to things I might have noticed otherwise.

I spent my first two years of college in the early 1980s playing D&D and dating a sizeable portion of the physics department at Washington University in St. Louis, Missouri, and my last two finding myself as an activist and a feminist. By the end of college, I had been engaged to a boyfriend for a whole, entire week and had gone to a lot of protests, women's collective meetings, and peace rallies. A lot of my friends came out at college, but I, determined to do things my own way, was straight until graduation.

I could say my coming out was the result of much soul-searching, followed by finding myself, but the truth was that I got drunk and fell into bed with a friend. I woke up happy, hungover, and crushed out. She woke up in love with someone else. I could say that at that point I used my heartbreak to begin rewriting my adolescence to reflect who I really was, recognizing my innate queerness in every gesture and clothing choice. But that wasn't what happened either.

Instead, I bounced around frenetically for a few days, burbling at friends, then followed that up with a fit of angst. A kindly gay friend loaned me Judy Grahn's *Another Mother Tongue* and his shoulder to process on. After that, my ex-boyfriend took me back after it became apparent that this woman that I thought I was falling in love with wasn't interested in me. Voila! I rediscovered myself as bisexual in less than a month.

It was more emotionally complicated than that, of course. I no longer felt straight, but I also didn't feel like I would only be attracted to women, forever and ever, amen. At the time, I thought this was the key requirement for identifying as a lesbian. Bisexuality felt like a better fit. It described how I felt about my relationships and how I responded to other people. I realized that I could be attracted to whomever I wanted to be, no longer boxed in by sex or gender, at least theoretically.

Could I have rediscovered myself as a lesbian? Possibly. I'd spent years organizing feminist events, volunteering in a women's bookstore collective, and taking women's studies classes. There was plenty of support available to me if I had wanted to identify as a dyke. In fact, there was plenty of social pressure for me to do so. Anything else was seen as suspicious, reflecting a lack of commitment and political backbone.

On the other hand, while some of my friends identified as bisexual, there were few bisexual resources in St. Louis in the mid-eighties. This only changed when one of the few out bi women I knew started a bi women's support group at the women's bookstore.

The store was contested ground. Collective meetings would periodically collapse into screaming matches over such topics as whether or not store newsletters should be mailed in brown paper wrappers so no one would be outed. Hosting a bi women's group was not wildly popular in this environment. But no one kicked us out. They just wouldn't date one of us.

So we held our meetings and our potlucks and were generally tolerated, if not loved. I was fairly oblivious since I wasn't sure how to go about dating girls to begin with.

In the meantime, I embraced feminism as a religion. It defined me. I hung out at women's dances, stopped shaving my legs, and became friends with some of the most outrageous dykes in the community. The charm of Meg Christian and Cris Williamson eluded me, but I could still sing "Leaping Lesbians" with the best of them. I fit in. Almost.

But it was still easier to date guys. I knew the rules. Granted, there was little subtlety to most of my relationships, many of them more one-night stands than anything else. My rare longer-term relationships were tumultuous, their passion extinguished by an excess of expectations and a steady loss of communication. One of my ex-boyfriends even told me after we broke up that he always expected me to dump him for a woman, perhaps one who existed only in my mind. He was right.

By that point, I was in my early thirties. I had tattoos and a shaved head, the souvenir of a crush on a friend. I ran the bi women's support group at the Women's Center at the University of Iowa and had my very own tiny feminist bookstore, Grassroots Books. I went to the occasional women's music festival and every Pride. I spoke to classes at the university about being bi, about being betwixt and between, about building an identity and a community on shifting sands.

Hanging around as the "token" out bisexual also meant that I got to hear a lot of bi trashing, some of it directed at me, some more general. When an acquaintance left her lover for a man, a mutual friend said, "We've lost another one." A lesbian coworker announced, "I've decided to stop hating you for being bisexual," in a way that suggested that I was supposed to be flattered. A kinder soul told me, "I know you say you're bisexual, but it's just easier to think of you as a lesbian."

Indeed. Sometimes it was easier for me too. I got in the habit of playing the "pronoun game," dragging out conversations for as long as I could without revealing the gender of my current lover. At the time, I thought I did this because I wanted to play with and confront assumptions about my sexuality. I enjoyed correcting people when they guessed wrong, enjoyed the speculation and verbal sparring that went on beforehand. In retrospect, it seems dishonest, more a function of the pressure I was under to conform than a real challenge to assumptions.

At the same time, it made me think about assumed monosexuality and how we learn to put people in boxes. Are you a girl or a boy? Gay or straight? Married or single? Even now, decades later, we're still wrangling with binaries.

Despite the word games and the way I was occasionally treated, I thought my work, beyond making me worthwhile as a human being, would bring me acceptance by the women's community I belonged to. Instead, I found that, if I wasn't careful, it made my bisexuality invisible. I was straight if I dated guys; I was a lesbian once I finally started dating women: not always, not consistently, but more often than I wanted to or should have. When I met my wife, a genuine "gold star" butch, and grew out my hair, that process escalated. I was part of the gang now: a real womyn among womyn (except for the whole butch/femme thing, which is a whole 'nother matter).

Don't get me wrong—I liked being a part of the lesbian community, even peripherally. I like the company of women and the sense of sisterhood it can give, however illusory it can sometimes be. It made me a lot of what I am today, giving me an independence and strength that I would have had a hard time finding otherwise. As a direct result of hanging out with lesbians and other queer women, I've had opportunities and relationships that helped me grow and I am grateful for what I learned, both good and bad.

But I find that I am still left conflicted, still feeling pulled in several directions. Despite my sense of otherness, I am, to all appearances, a lesbian now. I've lived with the same woman for over twenty years. We're married and monogamous and we own a house, complete with the requisite cats, furniture, and garden. I've become a writer who's primarily known for her writing about lesbians. The only thing standing between the "l" word and me is a desire to be honest with myself. The question is: what else can I call myself?

There are a lot more options than there used to be. But I want a word to call my own, and *byke* doesn't cut it. *Lesbian-identified bisexual* smacks of the academic. Someone I know identifies as *sovereign*, which has a nice ring to it but doesn't really describe how I feel about myself. *Other* comes closest in some ways but doesn't have the most positive connotations. Reflecting on it all gives me a sense of dislocation. Am I really bisexual if I only sleep with a woman? Am I really bisexual if most of my writing features relationships, sexual and otherwise, between women? What is a "real" bisexual anyway?

Contemplating my personal identity spills over into contemplating my personal community. When I first came out as bi, I felt isolated and wanted a bi community to call my own. I made do in the straight world, but I still wanted something else, something more. By the time I was in graduate school, I felt ready to try to build that community that I had always wanted. By then, I was one of the town's "performing out bisexuals." Back then, there were only three or four of us around to do the talks to the classes, to insist on including the "B" word in LGBTQ, to plan the potlucks.

But slowly, our numbers grew and it got a little easier. Soon there were other people to fight the good fight, to plan the meetings and floats at Pride. I looked at what they built and found that I didn't feel like I fit in there either. I don't mean that anyone made me feel unwelcome or even that I disagreed with what they were doing. Generally speaking, that wasn't and isn't the problem.

I don't live in those university towns anymore, and here in Minneapolis, where I live now, there is an organized bi community. But somehow, like identifying as a lesbian or as straight, it doesn't feel like home. I think some of it is big-picture stuff: a lot of the issues under discussion give me a sense of *déjà vu*. When I go to events, I feel like there's a greater emphasis on the process of coming out, on self-defining and support for the newly out or questioning, rather than on moving forward toward Bisexuality 3.0 or equivalent, variously defined.

Mind you, I know that isn't a completely fair criticism and I know that the 101/102 stuff is very important. And a lot of activists are working on the big picture and I do respect and actively support much of the work that is going on, but it's not necessarily what I get to see on the ground level.

This kind of organizing and processing isn't the only thing that stands between me and card-carrying bisexuality, truth be told. I'm still very woman-centered, for one thing, and I don't always feel there is room for that at the bi conferences and events that I've attended. It's as if I'm not "true bi," whatever that is. Given my background in lefty and feminist politics, it's also difficult for me to immerse myself in organizing around my sexual identity. For me, it's always "I'm bisexual and . . ." I keep looking for something more and I don't often find it.

On the other hand, one of the things I admire about the bi communities that I see now is their lack of rigidity. While I've heard BDSM, polyamory and monogamy, and related topics heatedly discussed, the separation between the groups hasn't really ossified. It's all still under construction. The really beautiful thing about building bi community is that like bisexuality itself there's so much flexibility and potential that it can go in any direction.

That said, I don't really know what I'm looking for in terms of community any more than I have a good word for what I feel myself to be. My personal community is a diverse lot of individuals whose identities range from staid heterosexuality to polymorphously perverse. The people I choose to hang around with tell me that maybe it's enough to accept and be accepted and not worry about the larger picture, the torturous twistings of LGBTQ+ politics and identity.

Maybe that's true. Maybe it's enough to make community where I find it and to play with the words, using them as tools, as building blocks. And so I will. I am a feminist, bisexual, middle-aged, fat, creative, and more. I'm happy to have made it this far, and to see some of the road ahead. Maybe it's enough to scrounge around outside and just be able to visit now and again. I don't know. Like my identity and my community, I'm still a work in progress.

JOSINA MANU MALTZMAN

Josina Manu Maltzman is a carpenter by trade, writer by passion, and rabble-rouser by everything else. Josina's essays can be found in *That's Revolting! Queer Strategies for Resisting Assimilation* (edited by Mattilda Bernstein Sycamore), *Walk Towards It* (edited by Ellen Marie Hinchcliffe), and elsewhere. An MFA candidate at Goddard College, Jo is working on a book-length mytho-biography titled *Dreaming Kaddish*.

On the Level

Biffys are my bathroom forty-plus hours a week. Jobsite portable toilets filled with blue liquid that freezes in the winter and becomes noxious boiling fumes in the summer. Unless it's been torn off or vandalized, the sticker inside the door announces, "Portable toilets save 148,000 gallons of water a day." Frequently there's graffiti staring back at me when I sit down: a huge cock scratched into the door, complete with ooze dripping out the hole in its tip, and next to that the words "out spics" or "KKK." I use my blade to scratch out the racist shit, then respond next to the deleted phrases with "FUCK YOU" and "NO RACISTS!" in jagged, pointy capitals. I leave the dick alone. The dense plastic that makes up the shitter box is difficult to scar, so I have to repeatedly etch it in order to leave my mark. It is disturbing that I have no idea if the dudes I work with did the graffiti or if the shitter arrived to my jobsite already decorated.

Safest to assume that it's the work of someone from my job.

As a white Jewish dyke carpenter named Jo, in my early mid-forties, with long brown hair on my head and stubble on my chin, I stand out on the jobsite. I ride a motorcycle when I'm not with my tools or my dog, and my scrappy faded tattoos are visible and plenty. If Jo from *The Facts of Life* spent her junior year on acid, then dropped out, that's me in a sitcom. I wear T-shirts that say things like "I Got Bat-itude!" I tell the guys, "Don't call me lady, but Sir will do just fine." I don't have to say I'm queer. Although I do talk about my partner, a bulldagger ten years my senior whom some people read as my dad on first glance.

I mostly work in new construction, on brand-new mansions built out in the suburbs. The setting is usually on a beautiful lake, with eagles dipping past the expansive windows while I work inside. I install cabinets, high-end, custom, sleek, and modern. Flip through the pages of *Dwell* magazine and that's what I do. These are homes for clients who can spend over a hundred thousand dollars on cabinets alone. Designer homes with spacious white walls bearing no art and cabinet surfaces unlittered with personal items. The cabinets are, in themselves, what is on display.

I got started in the trades almost twenty years ago, depending on how you count. I wasn't raised in the trades; on the contrary, I came from an academic family where thinking and writing were labors more respected than building or fixing. I was a stubborn wild child, nearly expelled from high school for truancy, who decided to stick with it and graduate because I saw it as my last free education. I had no intention of going to college. I had family who would gladly have paid for it, but it would have come at other costs. My distaste for education was not out of rebellion—I sincerely had no interest in the academy, nor could I see what it had to offer me. What I really wanted to be when I grew up was a tattoo artist.

I got my first tattoo at age sixteen at the only shop in Minneapolis at the time, a sleazy biker establishment called Tattoos by Yurkew. A year later Tatūs by Korē opened a few blocks down on Lake Street, and I went in for my second tattoo, soon followed by my third and fourth. Korē had an I-don't-give-a-shit attitude, and a way that was neither butch nor femme, but one hundred percent dyke. This made an imprint on me deeper than ink and was something I aspired to without understanding.

After much persuasion Korē agreed to let me apprentice with her, an ill-fated arrangement that lasted little over a year. My arrogance and impatience convinced me that I was ready to take my skills on the road. I bought an '82 Ford Club Wagon van, four-on-the-floor, to load with my tattoo equipment, a stovetop autoclave, and the rest of my belongings. I went first to Olympia, where I had a lover who was handy and built a bed for "Bessie" (yes, I named the van). They constructed a clever knockdown assembly that fit snugly into the back of the van.

At the time, I could not have built myself something as simple as a bed frame. I had no inclination toward carpentry, and my urge to throw a hammer when frustrated came often. During my travels I spent time in Colorado, on a plot of land that my friends bought. Those forty acres in the high desert were miles off the dirt road, miles off the paved road, and miles from the super max prison. When I arrived, my friends had just had the well dug and moved a double-wide trailer onto the property. The first building project was the well house/root cellar. It was my friend's ingenious design, post–architecture school. The materials arrived and I learned each step, the five of us toiling together on this big project, laying course after course of concrete block.

In Colorado, the lime and sand changed me. I started to think about the practicality of tattooing. I mean, when the shit goes down, what kind of skills would I have from being a tattoo artist? I would know what to do in the case of small surface wounds. I would know how to care for someone in stress and pain. I would know a bit about small electrics and DC power. All of these things could make someone very useful in an apocalypse or revolution, if they are the caring type, which I am not. . . . But *building* shit. Yes. If I were a carpenter I would know how things were built and I would have the skills to do it. Now *that* would be useful.

I decided to quit the road life and move to a city. I was determined to get a job in the trades, so I started by cold-calling want ads for laborers in the classifieds. I would dial and wait for someone to answer. I'd say, "Hello, I'm calling about the ad." They'd laugh and say, "You're a girl," and hang up. I became used to this, and more resolute. Eventually I met a couple who flipped houses. They hired people in the punk scene for labor and this was my way into the trades.

Since then I've worked in a variety of outfits, for employers and on my own, in multiple states. Early on there was a collective I formed in Philly with five other queers and gender deviants. We had little experience and a lot of chutzpah. We took on a few light renovation projects, but it was a short-lived endeavor. After that fell apart, I apprenticed with a trim carpenter in rural Virginia, working on a $12 million renovation. At 5:00 AM we'd start the drive to the jobsite through rolling foggy hills, slick with winter dew. On that first morning, as my new boss steered along swooping bends, he told me that giving blow jobs was part of my job description. I told him to fuck off just as he pulled up to the guard booth at the entrance to the estate. He signed us in as I looked around at the chef's house, the driver's house, and all the other buildings that made it look like a neighborhood, not a single property. My jaw would have dropped but I was not about to sit there with my mouth open.

That job didn't last very long.

Next I worked for a small company owned by a black man, and after that, another owned by a white lesbian where my coworkers were all Latinx—these situations are rare in the mostly segregated nonunion construction world. Both companies struggled to make ends meet and had a hard time getting paid for jobs and, consequently, a hard time paying their employees. They would frequently take state contracts for jobs that required a percentage of "minority"-owned companies and labor. These jobs seem to be great opportunities on the surface, meant to boost equity in employment in the trades, but they are mired in bureaucracy. It takes months for the state to issue payments, so small companies have to front the capital to keep everything running in the meantime, to the point of near collapse.

Now, as a subcontractor, my clients are the cabinet company whose products I install or the general contractor who is building the house. Technically I am self-employed, which means I hustle to make sure my work calendar is filled. I'm usually on a jobsite for four to six weeks installing the kitchen, the pantry, the bar, the office, the buffet, the main-level powder bath, the kids' bath, the master bath, the guest bath, the second bar, and sometimes a built-in in the master bedroom. It's a lot of cabinets to fill with belongings and crap from Costco.

By the time I arrive on a jobsite, most of the other subs are gone and I have the place to myself for the first week. The floor tile is set, the lighting and plumbing is roughed in, and the walls are primed. I usually have a luxurious week to blast my music, lunch in the quiet looking out on the lake, and work free from the dude-bro masculinity that dominates when other crews are around. After a few days of quiet, the place is a madhouse. Trim carpenters are riding my ass, painters are riding theirs. Stonemasons or tilers are in to finish the fireplace, and there is likely a lot of exterior work happening, even in deep winter.

I meet three types on a jobsite. The majority are white men who are immediately uncomfortable upon seeing me. They look, then look away, never making eye contact or introducing themselves. The second kind are men who, upon seeing me, get a twinkle in their eyes and instantly transform me into a walking hole for their dick, wondering if today will be their lucky day. The third kind of person is rare. This is the guy who doesn't bat an eye, who greets me like a human being, "Hey. How's it going." And then goes about his business or asks me questions without looking around for someone with a penis to answer it first. (*Don't assume I don't have a penis. Mine is just detachable.*)

I hate to admit it, but I've gotten used to the misogyny. My cardinal rules of survival are:

1. Never Let 'Em See You Bleed
2. You Have Nothing to Prove (but carry that heavy shit yourself)
3. You're Nobody's Sweetie and Nobody's Bitch
4. Thick Skin is Harder to Cut

Most of the homeowners love seeing a woman carpenter working on their new home. It's something they can brag about over cocktails. Sometimes I'm asked for my opinion on a design element, which I am ready to offer, unless it's about which shade of white for the walls—to which I reply that the front entry of my home is hot pink. What I don't tell them is that my first-floor bathroom is still charred from the squatter fire that happened before I bought the place, and hanging on an exposed stud in the upstairs bathroom is a print depicting golden showers. The purpose of walls is to display art, not just support a structure. In my home there are endless projects I wish to do, some maintenance and some aesthetic, all of them waiting for the money and time. Like the rest of my colleagues, I can't afford to live in the homes we build.

Unlike my colleagues, I constantly balance the reality of the work I do against my values. I earn my bread and butter by making homes pretty for the wealthy, and my skills have led me to work in a niche market that will likely thrive as this divide between the ultrarich and everyone else expands. I tune in to local and global politics, and I am sensitive to the realities of white supremacist and capitalist violence that many of the people I love deal with daily. My work is far from utilitarian and nothing revolutionary.

A few months ago I served a weekend in the Hennepin county jail, officially called the Work House. I negotiated a plea bargain of time in jail in order to avoid probation. I was arrested, along with over forty others, for protesting the murder of Philando Castile in July 2016. I, along with numerous others arrested over the summer, held off taking a plea to leverage our cases in support of another arrestee from a different demonstration who faced trumped-up felony riot charges. His crime: being a black man protesting the police murders of black men. Our collective pressure campaign succeeded. I took a guilty plea to a charge of public nuisance and was sentenced to a weekend of jail time.

On my second day, I was let out on work release. I was checked out of my cell before sunrise and spent the day at the lakeside jobsite dressing cabinets, a quiet Sunday all to myself. I drove myself back to jail, checked in, and waited for release. My next day back at work, one of the guys attempted to bond over being in jail. Apparently, word had gotten around. "Your reason is more noble than mine though. I was just drunk!" he kidded.

I gave him a half smile, accepting his gesture. But having nothing to say in response, I turned back to my work leveling a run of cabinets. Sometimes focusing on the task at hand is easier than facing the chasm of difference between the worlds I live in.

JOHN MEDEIROS

Originally from Providence, Rhode Island, John Medeiros is an award-winning writer, poet, and immigration attorney who now lives in Minneapolis. For nearly two decades, he shaped and co-curated the Queer Voices Reading Series that is the subject of this book. More information about him and his writing can be found at jmedeiros.net.

Losing Dylan

I could barely feel him in his last year, when Dylan put his arm around my shoulder. *If I have to think about it, the only thing I ever really loved was counting,* he said as he watched the clock on his nightstand as if he were listening to it, waiting for it to tell him a secret long kept. *You should leave. It's ten minutes to midnight.*

And he was telling the truth. By the age of three he could count to ten. And when he was eight years old, he knew every possible combination of whole numbers that brought him to that number. The number ten was a universe he completely dominated and easily controlled.

In junior high school he learned fractions and percentages and the decimal system, an entire language and culture based on the number ten. In high school he learned geometry and calculus, reinventing ways to count, rediscovering his journey back home to the same number.

Counting was his passion; it was the only way he knew how to love.

That is why, as he grew older, his fingers betrayed him and left him devastated. They took the soul he had as a child and cut it into tiny pieces and hid them among fire trucks and Legos. By the time he was twenty-five, his soul was fully haunted, ripened, lined with cobwebs and dead trees and all the things adult souls are made of before they turn into nothing.

Instead of a blinking streetlight, he saw darkness.

Instead of the laughter of children, he heard echoes.

How ironic to look back and say these things now, but they've always been true.

• • •

I've known him since the day he was born. As his cousin, I was there when his parents brought him home from the hospital; he was like a moth, wrapped in a cloud of yellow fleece.

He's so tiny, I remember thinking, my small, child's hand able to cover his face entirely.

I was with him in grade school, and I've seen him develop over the years, from the brainy student in junior high to the budding genius of a scientist in high school. Other students spent their days going to concerts and movies and hanging out at fast-food restaurants until it was time to go home, but Dylan was different.

As a teenager he always kept a journal. It contained the normal (and expected, by this time) mathematical formulas and scientific notations, but it also contained some of the most disturbing poems and drawings I had ever seen. I felt distant, yet at the same time I knew him in a way no one else did.

I suppose, in a way, I despised being his cousin because, deep down, I wanted only to be a part of the ethereal world that eventually embraced him.

It was while he was in high school when he started to delve into that mysterious land of dark shadows and imaginary spirits that seemed to later possess him. Whenever I caught him talking aloud in full conversation, no one else in the room and eyes fixed in a gaze that took him to universes outside his window, I would ask him who he was talking to.

His response was always the same: *The friends you are not allowed to see, so don't bother asking.*

The spells became more frequent, and that was when the doctors examined him for the first time. And though it would be years before an official diagnosis, they warned us that hallucinations were not unusual. *He needs love,* was all they would tell us. *We don't know much about what is happening to him, but one thing we know for certain—he needs to learn to love, and he needs to learn to be loved. That will help make him feel whole and complete.*

Whole and complete. I think it was then that I felt real love for him for the first time.

The fact that we were both men didn't scare me. The fact we

were cousins scared me even less. What frightened me more than anything else was that since the day he was born, it was as though Dylan was fading away from us, and no matter how I tried, I could not penetrate him. He was like a room with no door. A wall made of cast iron. A stone.

If there's any crying to be done, I'll be the first to do it, he would later say when we first found out about his diagnosis. *And if anyone was going to feel sorry for me, it would be me and me alone.* He whispered this from beneath the covers of his bed when I slept over, half the person I remember him being, sleeplessness and despair hidden in shades of yellow.

He was nineteen when I noticed that his eyes had grown black— they would later say that is the first physical sign with this disease. Throughout our childhood they were always blue, but it was only when we were in college—he, a freshman, I, a senior—when his eyes slowly started to change to a darker shade of green before turning black completely. I tried to ask him about it one day, lying next to him on his bed, holding him as if I were a surrogate mother and he a foster child. I tried to warn him as one might try to stop a train from running. It was that futile.

Dylan, the blue in your eyes is almost gone, I said, running my fingers through his hair the way a mother might do. *Have you ever noticed that?*

Yes, but I can still see, was his only reply.

And I remember that moment as if it were just yesterday. Going back to my dorm room that evening after he fell asleep I asked out loud to no one, *Why does every second feel like the last, as if the moment I leave his side the next bomb will fall, or the sky will turn to ash and bury us alive? Why are my thoughts always like captive birds, my words like sad prison songs?*

These were the questions of a prisoner losing his cellmate, my cell just a thought and a room away. And as I walked inside my world as if nothing else existed in it, secretly he walked around with me, haunting those walls, reminding me that my life sentence had already begun, that life both stops and carries on, that the minutes pass by without parole, without any relief other than his smile and his words as they fell like flower petals from his lips.

The diagnosis finally came one year later, and when it did, neither of us could believe it. *Invisibility?* we asked the doctors incredulously.

It's hard to believe, and to this day doctors cannot completely explain it, but since the day of his birth Dylan has suffered from an illness without a name. Simply put, he is becoming involuntarily invisible, slowly but steadily with each passing year.

To understand this phenomenon, it helps to appreciate the basic principles of physics. Objects are seen when light reflects off their surfaces. In its simplest form, invisibility occurs when objects no longer reflect light. This stage is called transparency. But before an object can become transparent, it must first go through a stage of translucence, where light is allowed to pass through it but does so diffusely, so it cannot be clearly seen through.

Dylan once told me, *Think of tinted glass that loses its color and becomes a frosted windowpane. Over time, it becomes clear, like glass. Only when the light has completely consumed the glass is the glass no longer visible.*

In Dylan's case, his disease caused his body—from his cells to his muscles and even his bones—to pass through a stage where he had become translucent. His image was still there, though it was vague and cloudy.

Am I beginning to lose you? I asked, not knowing what to expect.

Lose me? he asked as if the question did not warrant merit.

I had to remind myself that he won't be dead, that wavelengths of light would begin to shift at a frequency outside the normal optical spectrum. Then, he won't be seen or heard, ever again.

What I learned over the years is that when the body becomes invisible, it does not do so overnight, and it does not occur finger by finger, limb by limb. Instead, this is the way it happens:

In an attempt to separate itself from the body, the mind hallucinates, as if it knows the body will soon disappear, so it spends its time finding a new home for itself. Color is the first thing to go away. The eyes turn pitch-black, giving credence to the belief that black is the absence of color and not the combination of all colors. The same is true with hair, just before it falls out. The blood then becomes clear, as if it were only plasma, and thins itself as it runs its course through the body. The loss of pigment in the skin then follows, and the body becomes pallid and must be protected from the sun.

Only when all color has gone does the light begin its slow ascent.

Then slowly—so slowly that it almost goes unnoticed—the body simply begins to fade all at once as light passes through it more intensely with each passing day, as if the body were a chalk mark left in the rain. As it does, the body becomes lighter in weight, its outlines more blurred and difficult to see, until it presents itself like a mist just before saying goodbye.

I say this because the very last thing to go is the voice.

At times this sounds unbelievable, but at other times it makes so much sense, as when I am on a plane and it passes through clouds and causes turbulence. Clouds remind me of Dylan because they, too, are somewhere between empty space and physical matter, almost unseen by the human eye, but very much in existence. Enough to shake a plane. Enough to shake my entire body.

Is it the mindlessness of childhood that opens up the world? Because today nothing happens in a gas station. This he said as we stopped to get gas before heading on a weekend camping trip to northern Minnesota. When he said things like this my world would suddenly stop, and I was reminded that our time together is sacred, and each moment— each carefully sewn moment—must be held in my hand and cherished like a fine, silk tapestry.

Today nothing happens in a gas station. I wanted to bottle that moment and preserve it forever. He loved to count, but I loved him most when his mind worked words this way. His illness was something I had grown used to, but over time loving him meant loving only a fragment of him, never loving the entire person completely. And though I desperately wanted him to get better, it was his mind I was most afraid of losing. So as his body slowly left him his mind never did, and I came to love that mind because it was the only part of him left to love; it was the only part of him that mattered.

I no longer thought of him as my cousin, but as a soul mate. A partner in life, however brief that life may be. Of course, I told no one because no one would understand, but I came to love him as a lover.

And I remember the first time we made love. Nothing scared me like his body that night. His hair had already fallen out, and his eyes were black and soft skin white. Afraid of himself, he asked me to hold him. And when I did, he said, *I feel like a clamshell bending in half, testing my strength as I test my hinge. I feel undone.*

And I remembered the words of his doctors: *Only through love would he feel complete.* So that night, under the canopy of the Minnesota sky, we made love, each completing the other.

Eventually, it would not be enough.

That was late October. Nearly four weeks passed after that incident, and he avoided me at all costs. At Thanksgiving the only real words he said were related to food.

Dylan seems to be angry with you for some reason, my aunt said to me when Dylan got up to go to the bathroom. *Is there something going on between you two?*

Nothing that should make him angry, was my reply. And that was exactly how I felt.

That night I wrote him a letter. Like a seed that needs nine days to grow, my thoughts began to take root on the tenth day. This is what I wrote: *It wasn't epilepsy, because epilepsy was never like this. Granted, your body jerked in convulsions as if you had an electrical storm raging inside you, and your eyes rolled into their sockets like two cameras eager to take a snapshot of you from the inside, the way I see you. But all that stopped the moment I removed my lips from your shoulder and kissed it and cupped it in the palm of my hand as it quivered like a lost bird and I whispered in your ear, 'Everything will be alright.'*

The first rule with epileptics is to keep the mouth open. Watch the tongue to make sure the victim does not swallow it accidentally. But it was my tongue he swallowed. My mouth he pried open to retrieve the sweet, magical elixir reserved only for him.

I wrote this only once I was completely consumed by him. Never had such an experience moved me so powerfully. The electricity of his body scared me at first, as if he lost control of his reflexes.

But what I was trying to tell him was that he did not lose control; instead he gave it to me, trusting me with it as one trusts his most intimate lover. The effect was still the same, but the passion made all the difference. It was not the loss of control, as with epilepsy, but something more, like love—a love too little, too late.

He later called to tell me the letter disturbed him because I compared our lovemaking to a disease.

I spent the next few months trying to determine what had the greatest effect on me: making love to the softness of his skin as his body fluttered beneath mine, or kissing away the tears that leaked from his eyes as he told me he wanted desperately to love me but didn't know how. *I feel half empty,* he said, but what does this mean when it comes from someone who is half visible?

Making love to him felt comfortable and natural, as if we were completely alone in our own private Eden. It felt that new. Maybe he wanted me to say, *I love you,* but I could not. Not because I did not feel love, but because saying so would be like trying to squeeze a lifetime of emotion into three tiny words—a cruel and unjust minimization. Instead I let my body speak for itself. My fingertips. My lips.

Do you know what is happening to us? I asked between kisses.

What? he asked.

We are communicating on a level far beyond the physical. I said this because the physical, we had come to learn, no longer mattered.

Why are we doing that? Dylan asked, the confusion gripping him only slightly.

Because I am trying to save you.

And he smiled for the first time since his diagnosis, and said, *I'm fading, yet with you I feel as impervious as scarlet.*

These were the last words he said. And as he said them, I reminded him that he was named after one of the greatest poets our world has ever known. One who wrote, *Do not go gentle into that good night. Rage, rage against the dying of the light.*

It has been nearly six months since he faded away; apparently, my love was not enough to keep him with me. It is now twilight, and the only light is the moon as its fingers slide through the window shades and point to the cobwebs on the ceiling and to the chair in the corner and to the mirror that sends them dancing on all four walls in a frenzied cabaret.

These, not people, are the things that reflect light.

Within the family we refer to the incident as the *loss of Dylan*, but I think that sounds as if we misplaced him. As if it were completely appropriate to say, *He was here a minute ago, and now he's gone*.

After all, this couldn't be less true, but how do you grieve the loss of someone who has not really died?

How do you make love to a shadow?

But we didn't really lose him at all. The doctors remind us that Dylan has moved into another dimension, one that allows him to see and hear us, although we are not allowed to see and hear him. This is worse than losing him, because there is still room for words in this place, so I must work overtime to *not* tell him the things I want to say:

That I see him in the eyes of complete strangers.

That I hear his voice when no one else is around.

That I am jealous of the loneliness that surrounds him.

And that in his last few weeks I wanted nothing more than to be the empty chair by his bedside, the echo of his voice in the hallway.

Instead I remain as silent as the light waves between us.

NASREEN MOHAMED

Nasreen Mohamed, a queer, gender-nonconforming Muslim born in Tanzania, calls the Twin Cities his home. As a Josie R. Johnson award recipient for his social justice and human rights effort at the University of Minnesota, Nasreen centers his writing in his third-world perspective, understanding that resistance is survival, truth is a lived experience, and liberation is another word for love.

Skipping Stones

Lailah haila La, La ilha, Haila Mohamed Du rasoolula.
I bear witness that there is no god, but Allah, and I bear witness that
*   Mohamed is the Messenger of Allah.*

I skip a stone on this still blue water,
It jumps up in the air to land on another still wave,

Catapulted back in the air,
It skips again and again and I count intently till it drowns to the
    bottom,

I no longer see it and will never see it again,
The drowned stone is you, Farkhunda Malikzada.

Farkhunda Malikzada, I have been carrying,
your story in my heart for the last six months,
this incident of your death spread through the world
to make the *New York Times* front-page story
and that's how you landed in my backpack.

They pulled off your hijab
and stoned you to death because
you exposed holy men for trafficking charms
and Viagra at the shrine,
They planned to get rid of you
by accusing you of burning a Quran,

a blasphemous act that would teach you
a lesson, so they could continue business as usual.

As the stones rained
over you, you fought back in red terror while people watched,
you believed
the god that protected you,
would not create
the violence that ultimately extinguished the dim
light that you held on to.

The story reads about the barbarism
of the incident,
The backward justice system
that would let
the men go
who caused your death,
Surprisingly, it showed a photograph of women with faces painted
    red,
like yours
in the last moments
of your life, carrying
your coffin
in defiance of thousands of years of tradition
that reserved this right to carry the dead
only for men,

The newspaper portrayed Muslim
women as fighters who put their bodies
on the front line,
but we know that
women have always been
on the front line.

I struggle with my own numbness
and fragility
to take your story

into my body,
You know
how we want to cover up
everything that is real
because we fear breaking apart,

We believe our numbness will protect us,
until the blood spilled is ours
for the lies that are the new
truth murder us
all, eventually.

I take a second stone and skip it,
trying to get more skips,
forcing the jumps to more life than it has,
it lands at the bottom, never to be seen, again.

For another stone drowned: Sandra Bland.
I wonder who saw you
and witnessed
your last breath,
for some reason, as I have been carrying the story
of Farkhunda Malikzada,
I see you
in persistent sunflowers growing
amidst cracked cement,
you defied orders for your vision
saw the injustice so clearly,
like those sunflowers that stubbornly raise themselves
to face the glorious sun,
you lived your life in rebellion without caution,
the system that relentlessly pursued
your death
has no indictment to its name
as the hashtag "say her name" continues
to light up our consciousness,
I wonder, to prove that something is not right

about our world, why do murders
have to grab headlines,

I take another stone and another and another and another for the
Transgender men and women murdered in 2017.

Mesha Caldwell, 41, a black transgender woman from Canton,
Mississippi, found shot to death the evening of January 4. She was
a popular beautician and makeup artist with a talent for creating
hairstyles in Crayola colors: curls the shade of burgundy wine, teal
mermaid-style waves that tumbled down her back, a glossy purple
bang falling over one eye. On her memorial Facebook page, a friend
jokingly lamented her edges and implored Mesha to send updates
about her hair down from heaven.

Jamie Lee Wounded Arrow, 28, an American Indian woman who
identified as transgender and two-spirit, found murdered in her
apartment in Sioux Falls, South Dakota. She was an active member
of the Sioux Falls Two-Spirit and Allies group. She worked in customer service and loved to spend her free time at the library. Friends
remember her as an honest, compassionate person who made an im-
pact on those who met her.

JoJo Striker, 23, a transgender woman, killed in Toledo, Ohio, on
February 8. Striker's mother, Shanda Striker, described her as "funny
and entertaining" and said her family loved her deeply.

Jaquarrius Holland, 18, shot to death in Monroe, Louisiana, on February 19. A friend described her "like a younger sister" and had helped
her learn to accept herself.

Tiara Richmond, 24, fatally shot in Chicago on the morning of February 21. A transgender woman of color, she was found dead on the
same street where two other transgender women were killed in 2012.
She was an advocate for transgender rights with Brave Space Alliance
in Chicago.

Chyna Doll Dupree, 31, a Black transgender woman, shot and killed in New Orleans on February 25. Chyna was a much-loved performer in the ballroom community who was visiting friends and family in New Orleans at the time of her death.

Ciara McElveen, 26, a transgender woman of color, stabbed to death in New Orleans on February 27. McElveen did outreach for the homeless community.

Alphonza Watson, 38, shot and killed in Baltimore, Maryland, on March 22. Watson's mother said her daughter was "the sunshine of our family," a "caring, passionate" person who loved cooking and gardening.

Kenne McFadden, 27, found in the San Antonio River on April 9. A high school friend of McFadden described her to local media as assertive, charismatic, and lovable.

Chay Reed, 28, a transgender woman of color, shot and killed on April 21 in Miami. Reed's longtime friend described her as someone who was full of life and beloved by many.

Kenneth Bostick, 59, found with fatal injuries on a Manhattan sidewalk. His friend described him as "the kindest, sweetest, gentlest person that I have ever had the pleasure to know." She wrote: "My sweet friend, I hope you are on a beach somewhere, having that fruity umbrella drink you talked about, and feel more at peace than you ever did in this life."

Sherrell Faulkner, 46, a transgender woman of color, died on May 16 of injuries sustained during an attack on November 30, 2016, in Charlotte, North Carolina. Sherrell was a force. According to a family friend, she wasn't afraid of any man because she had been shot on several occasions and gotten right back up. "When she loved, she loved hard."

Kendra Marie Adams, 28, found in a building that was under construction. She is described as a "beautiful person" who was charismatic and "always joking around with her friends."

Ava Le'Ray Barrin, 17, shot and killed in Athens, Georgia, on June 25. In an online obituary, friends remembered Ava as a "social butterfly" and an "amazing girl" who "loved to make people laugh."

Ebony Morgan, 28, shot multiple times in Lynchburg, Virginia, in the early morning of July 2. She was a mother who is described as having a gorgeous smile.

TeeTee Dangerfield, 32, a Black transgender woman, shot and killed on July 31 in Atlanta, Georgia. By all accounts, Dangerfield was defying the odds of many trans women of color, who are systematically discriminated against. She had a good union job at the airport, she had her own home, and she had recently bought a brand-new Dodge Challenger. But according to her best friend, there was one other thing on her list that she wanted: "She wanted children, she wanted to get married, she wanted a lover."

Gwynevere River Song, 26, shot and killed in Waxahachie, Texas, on August 12. "My daughter was incredibly smart," their mother said. "An avid reader of current and past historical events, their mind was like a sponge full of knowledge in many topics. Great debater! They were beautiful, caring to the point they carried others' burdens within themself."

Kiwi Herring, 30, killed during an altercation with police on August 22. A neighbor described her as giving, saying, "If you needed anything from Kiwi, she would give it to you. She'd see my kids outside playing and she'd hand out popsicles, have barbecues, all that."

Kashmire Nazier Redd, 28, transman fatally stabbed by his partner on September 5 in Gates, New York. A friend said in a Facebook post, "He was ambitious, strong willed, and self-driven. No matter what he went through he still came out on top. He loved hard and all he ever wanted was to be loved and accepted."

Derricka Banner, 26, shot to death in Charlotte, North Carolina, on September 12. Friends describe Banner as a "playful spirit" and a "go-getter" who enjoyed life.

All of them transgender,
women and men murdered,
just this year. I carry them
inside me
for I know
that could easily have been me.

My heart and my arm are hurting
having to continuously skip
in memoriam and feeling the weight of grief
in this poem, for I have not even begun
to skip stones for those unknown bodies that will never be
mentioned in any poem or make headlines.

I want to end this poem on an optimistic note
and tell you that we are winning this fight,
that our social media likes and shares are making a difference,
when I know that knowledge does not change the world,
But I want to leave us disturbed with the sadness
and loss for just this moment,
to feel the pain of interrupted lives,

We are satisfied being peddled hope, the language of complacency
and protection that this is someone else's pain
and grief to carry, until we see
our dead body and the body of a loved one,

So I ask us to bear witness and feel this pain
so we may not ignore
and look away at the riverbanks that carry our dead.

MICHAEL KIESOW MOORE

Michael Kiesow Moore is the award-winning author of the poetry collection *What to Pray For*. His work has appeared in several books and journals, he founded the Birchbark Books Reading Series, and he dances with the Ramsey's Braggarts Morris Men.

The Day I Recognized that the Country Turned Against Me, Again

It was an unpleasant feeling, been a while since I felt this.

I was driving across Wisconsin, returning to my home in Saint Paul from a visit with family. I stopped for gas. As I walked from the convenience store, I saw that I was surrounded by men almost twice as large as me, wearing orange hats and hunter camouflage green. Suddenly I was conscious of my car's Human Rights Campaign and rainbow-colored peace sign bumper stickers. I wore a long Italian black winter coat and a dapper maroon-colored scarf. The thought arrived, "all these men probably voted for Trump." I did not feel safe. I remembered a time many years ago when a man brandished a knife at me, saying, "I'm going to kill the faggot." That was not likely to happen here, at a gas station parking lot, but I did feel eyes upon me—I felt noticed, thoughts running through these men's heads that I was not one of them. This is not my country anymore, again.

AHMAD QAIS MUNHAZIM

Ahmad Qais Munhazim is a PhD candidate in political science at the University of Minnesota. His research focuses on issues of international human security, political violence, vigilant masculinities, gender and sexuality, migration, and feminist and queer Muslim movements.

A Letter from Exile

Beloved Mother,

I write you this letter in the middle of a cold Minnesota night. The winters are very harsh here but somehow I have gotten used to them. The heat is on right now but my feet are cold and my body numb. I don't know if it is the crack in the window or the thunder inside my chest that is shaking my body like a dead dry leaf on the ground. Every night when I lay my tired head on the pillow, I think of you and everyone at home. I think of your kind, loving heart that longs for your four kids who are oceans away from you, in foreign lands where nobody wants them. Nobody wants them, mother. You just hear their voices behind the phone and see them in your dreams from time to time. I see you in my dreams quite often too but I don't tell you because I know you will miss me even more and cry behind the phone.

When I read the news on suicide bombings in Kabul, I think of your kind hands that might be protecting my seven little nephews and nieces. You protected me and my siblings when we were little. You would hold me under your chadar when the sound of war scared me. You gathered us in your arms and sat in the cold corner of our basement until the screeching sound of rockets hitting our neighborhood faded away. You would tell us to walk out of the basement one at a time when they announced cease-fire for a few hours. We knew that you couldn't lose all of us together. You walked first and we lined up behind you, just like the duck in our neighborhood and her little babies.

Mother, I am scared to sleep tonight. What if I wake up to a raid in my room and my half-naked brown body is dragged by immigration officers on the floor? People say that the government has started raiding homes and detaining immigrants. Mother, do you remember when we were refugees in Pakistan, and they would come and raid our house in the middle of the night? You always knew when they were coming. The second you heard the sound of the police Jeep, you would send us to the rooftop and tell us to stay there until the dawn. I broke my ankle that one night when I jumped off the roof, right when the police got there. Back then I was only fourteen and ankles healed fast. I am getting old now. I don't think it will heal fast. Neither can I go to the rooftop here. They don't allow residents to go on the rooftops.

Mother, I am scared to sleep. What if I wake up to news of another suicide bombing in Kabul? I stop breathing every time I scroll through the news and read about another bomb, another drone in my sweet home, Afghanistan. I am scared that they would come for you this time. I can't lose you. You are all I have. I already lost my dad. You never told me what happened to my dad, and to this day I speak of him in present tense. You lost someone you had spent fifty years of your life with. I am still ashamed of myself for not being able to attend his funeral. I was afraid they wouldn't renew my student visa, wouldn't allow me to come back and continue with my studies. They had already started vetting Afghans and Iraqis. They had already refused visas for many students who had gotten scholarships and had crafted their dreams for a happy future. I was too afraid to see my dreams shatter.

Mother, I am scared when I walk out these days. I heard they have been attacking Muslims in different cities. I don't blend or hide in the crowds well. My brown body burns with the shame of not belonging. When I cover my body, my thick accent gives it away. *Where are you from? How did you get here? No, seriously? Do you have documents?* they ask me casually. *You have an accent*, they add. I wish I could tell them that the smoke bombs of their drones threw me out here. But instead, my voice shakes, "Afghanistan." They take a step back. Everything goes silent. They try to gather their freshly shaken white thoughts. They don't want to lose their "Minnesota Nice." The face they gave me is as if I am the one droning. They look me up and down like they are the drop-out-of-high-school TSA at the airport trying to decide whether my queer body should go through a strip search or a body scan to prove that I am not a threat to their national security. *You speak good English.* Yes, they approve of my English at the corner grocery store, on the bus, at the bank, when I check out a book or I buy a shirt. They gave me a colonial stamp on my thick accent. I smile like I used to nine years ago when I landed here.

Mother, I am scared I will never be able to see you again. I will never be able to forgive myself. I haven't seen you in five years. And, wallahi, you haven't been away from my eyes or my mind, not even for a second. My heart bleeds every time I hear you behind the phone crying about how much you miss me. I miss you too, Mother. I miss you so much that every Friday I go to the nursing home and hang out with other people's moms and grandmas. I push their wheelchairs to the park. We sit under the tall trees or in the nearby coffee shop and I paint their nails. They tell me they don't like Muslims or refugees. I smile and I do not tell them I am both Muslim and refugee. I don't want them to stop me painting their nails. I wouldn't be able to see their hands colorless and nails sad and cracked.

With Love,
Your son in exile

Tonight the Subject Is Love

Farsi, my native language, is gender-neutral. Yes, while heterosexual white men in the west are upset over all-gender restrooms, my language was developed gender-neutral five thousand years ago . . . but hey, you still call me third-world, barbaric, backward, caveman. Anyway, the gender-neutral beauty of Farsi allowed me to sometimes write poems about my crushes, longing, and pain, about men—and not give anyone reasons to question my sexuality. I wasn't wearing shiny shoes, glittered pants, or floral bags back then. So, stop staring at me like, "Queen, please! How the hell did you fool them?" I was quite butch. I mean, until I talked, walked, or danced. I wrote poems deep in the nights while the moon witnessed—every night, regardless of rockets flying or bombs dropping. I stayed up and wrote poems so that I could read them to Mahmood after work the next day. It was our little romantic routine, except that I ruined this romantic fling with poems about war, pain, and separation. He would come at 7:00 PM sharp to pick me up, and we would drive slowly around Kabul, over empty streets, dark broken roads, but under a sky full of stars and a bright, happy moon. As we played our favorite romantic songs in the background, I would open my diary and read my new poems.

"The subject tonight is love," I whispered sheepishly to Mahmood sitting next to me, as I opened my worn-out red diary with its pages falling apart and cover split in half.

Mahmood, while holding the steering wheel with one hand, reached to turn down the volume of our favorite Bollywood song: *Lag jaa gale ke phir yeh haseen raath ho na ho. Shaayad phir is janam mem mulaaqat ho na ho* (Hug me, for who knows if this beautiful night will ever come again. Maybe, in this life, we may or may not meet again). "Go ahead and read; I am listening," Mahmood declared with a smile on his face and the usual flirt in his eyes telling me he knew the subject was not just love, it was our love. "But wait! What happened today, your subject is love? It is usually war," Mahmood added.

"Love is the other side of war. Today with all the war engulfing this city, I just want us to drive around our broken Kabul and scream poems of love," I murmured.

Earlier today, the streets were filled with screams, cries, gunshots, sounds of tanks, shatterings of glasses, and blood of street vendors being run over by the American soldiers on their morning patrol. I was stuck for nine hours in the basement of our office with eighty other people, hearing the gunshots, machine guns, screams of protesters outside as we locked ourselves in our privileged, secure UN compound. The American soldiers were drunk at 7:00 AM as they got on their colonial machines, starting off their daily check on the savage people of their little colonies. They left the military base in Bagram, north of Kabul, but less than a mile down the road they started running over fruit vendors, imprinting their colonized bodies on the broken asphalt roads of western democracy and freedom. More than a hundred people were slaughtered under their tanks as the American boys laughed, lifted up their beers, and made their way down to Kabul. As they got to Kabul, people tried to stop them, but they fired their Second Amendment and shot down many unarmed protesters. Kabul's street looked like the zombie pub crawl young white Minnesotans celebrate in the month of October, fetishizing death and romanticizing blood and violence. Today war was everywhere, so I didn't want it to appear in my poems again. I just wanted the rest of the night to be about love.

Is it love?
The waiting.
Long hours of aching.
Feeling alive a moment
The next agony and suffering
Is it a forbidden love?
Am I forbidden?
Are you forbidden?
Love . . .

A heavy thump on the windshield, and Mahmood lost control of the steering wheel, screaming at me, "Get down under the seat." Before I could, the car came to a sudden stop by hitting something stiff and still. My head crashed against the car's roof and I heard Mahmood yelling, asking if I was okay. "What was it?" I whispered with my shaky voice, holding my head tight with my palm, feeling the warm flow of blood.

Before Mahmood could answer, flashlights blurred my eyes. "Do not move!" the American soldier commanded as he opened the door on my side. I saw a tank full of soldiers parked by our car. And our car standing right in front of a giant willow tree. "Why didn't you stop when we told you to stop with our laser light? Are you fucking blind? Do you speak English?" the soldier yelled at Mahmood.

"Sorry we not see you or the light we just headed home, my friend hurt," Mahmood told the soldier with his broken English.

"Next time you do not stop, we will shoot you. You got lucky this time; we only threw a bottle of vodka at your car." As he told us what hit our car that made us crash into the tree, his fellow soldier friend screamed, "They were probably doing some Muslim fag shit in there; that's why they couldn't see us."

"You don't see us next time, you are dead, bro," the soldier yelled as he slammed the door and they walked back to their tank.

My head healed. Two years passed. My plane landed in Minneapolis. It was like being born all over again but this time as a big, giant, adult child. I looked for people with dark hair whenever I needed directions. The doors confused me: I would pull them when they said push. I never got them right. Why do these doors have to be so complicated? Can there be just one way to open them? I always wondered as I got closer to a door. I opened the door to the computer lab at University Village and saw a woman in hijab. It was like opening the door to my home. I walked up to her and said, "Salam alaikum."

She smiled and said, "Walaikum asalam. Are you a new student? I am Yusra." The five-foot-tall woman with a pink floral hijab and light purple lipstick greeted me as she reached to shake my hand. Yusra became my human Google and my first friend in Minnesota. I would run to her if I needed directions how to get to my orientation class or how to operate a laundry machine.

"I will walk you to your first class. It is in Blegen Hall 120," Yusra assured me as we both got on the Campus Connector. We got to my human rights class a bit early. Yes, very unlike me and Muslims in general. Yusra left for her class and I started to feel nervous. I plugged in my headphones and listened to my favorite song, *Lag Ja gale ke phir yeh haseen raath ho na ho.* As the seats started to fill up, the professor arrived. We got the syllabus and the professor went on to explain each weekly topic. When he finished reading, he asked if there were any other topics we wanted to add onto the syllabus.

I waited for others to raise their hands, as I did not want to be the first and I was very nervous and unsure about my English. I didn't want to embarrass myself, but nobody raised their hands. I raised my hand and requested to have a week dedicated to discussing the US wars and their implications for human rights. As I was saying this, my voice started to shake and I began to stutter and I heard murmurs and whispers.

The professor nodded and called on a student who was interrupting me to speak louder. "I am just saying, go back to your country if you think the US is a human rights violator. Why are you here then?" All the heads turned toward me and my head turned toward the back of the class to see who said that. The tall, young, white guy in military uniform staring at me continued, "I am talking to you."

I turned my head back to the professor, waiting for his reaction or just a mere gesture of empathy, but he simply ignored my existence and continued reading the next page on the syllabus. I didn't want him to kick the student out of the class or create a scene. All I wanted was empathy, because caring for others and their pain is a radical act of love. One doesn't need to pick up a rifle to start a revolution against the oppressor. Sometimes empathy is revolutionary.

Sometimes my existence itself is a radical act.

GARY ELDON PETER

Gary Eldon Peter's stories have appeared in *Callisto, Alexandria Quarterly, Water~Stone Review, Great River Review,* and other publications. His short fiction collection, *Oranges,* won the 2016 New Rivers Press Many Voices Project competition in prose and was published in 2018.

More Than a Feeling (an excerpt)

"Algebra, Spanish, history," Andy snorts. "Who needs this shit?" He spins his *¡En español!* textbook like a Frisbee across the room until it hits the wall with a thud.

You do, if you ever want to make it out of the tenth grade. But of course I just nod, agreeing with everything Andy says. It's become a bad habit, like smoking or an unhealthy food you can't give up. But I can't help myself. Because if it makes Andy smile, a smile that says *Yes, it's you and me, we're in something together*, then it's worth it.

It's Sunday afternoon, with only two weeks to go until Thanksgiving recess, and I've gotten permission to spend it with Andy so we can study our Spanish together. Except for school, Andy's been grounded for the last month because of his bad midterm grades.

Even though the whole point was to study together, and therefore do better in school, my father wasn't crazy about me spending any more time with Andy than I already was. "I think it might be a good idea for you to expand your friendship circle a little bit," he said one cold morning when we were out doing chores, not long after Andy's last visit at our place to work on algebra. "Aren't there other guys you might want to do things with?"

Don't get worked up, I thought as I kept my head down and shoveled more feed for the cows. *Play it cool.*

"It's just not . . . healthy to spend all your time with one friend. Why not broaden your horizons a bit?"

"Okay," I had said, trying to sound noncommittal. I wasn't about to give up Andy. And just as I'd hoped, after some additional bullshitting about how tutoring would be good for me too, since by having to explain it to someone else I'd do better, my father didn't bring it up again. That was a little risky, since he'd been a teacher himself before we started farming and he could have easily seen that I had no clue what I was talking about. But then again maybe he knew it was a lost cause.

"What are you doing for Thanksgiving?" I ask Andy now. Given Andy's short attention span, I've learned that it works best to ease slowly into tutoring: a little bit of small talk first, then on to "Basic Conversations."

Andy shrugs. "The usual shit. We'll eat a lot, and then I'll goof around with my cousins. Last year my uncle let me have a couple beers. He poured it into an empty pop can and so my dad didn't even know."

"What happened after that?"

"I got tired, and then I had to pee really bad," Andy says. "That was about it. You need to have a lot before you feel anything. My uncle and dad usually have to drink a whole twelve pack before anything happens to them."

"So what do they do after that?"

"Not much. Act stupid, mostly, and be loud. The more they drink, the louder they get. My dad yells at my mom for no reason. Or at me. Sometimes that's kind of funny. But it's not like he's ever hit her, or anything. Or me. Sometimes drunk people do that, but he never has. If he ever took a swing at me, I'd give him a couple of these." Andy gets up from the floor and dances from side to side, like a boxer, occasionally throwing a punch, but after about thirty seconds he gets tired and sits back down on the floor. "So what are you going to do?"

"We'll be at my great-aunt Magda's in Mankato—me, my little sister, my dad, and Miss Nesbit."

"Who's Miss Nesbit?"

"She lives with my aunt."

My great-aunt Magda, my grandmother's sister on my mother's side, has never been married. She's lived with Rosemary Nesbit for over thirty years. Miss Nesbit, as I had been taught to call her (to call her "Rosemary" would not have been polite, my mother told me, no matter how long they had lived together and how well we knew her), taught civics and retired the same year Aunt Magda did from her job as a world history teacher at the same high school. Every year, for as long as I can remember, we've spent Thanksgiving at their house.

They're a couple. A *couple* couple.

When I was nine my mother sat me down and explained it all to me: how they loved each other in the same way that a man and a woman could love each other, and that was fine, people could love whomever they wanted and it wasn't up to us to judge. But she didn't have to tell me anything, because I had already figured it out way before that. You could tell it by the way they were with each other. It was hard to explain.

"What does your aunt's friend look like? Is she a fox?"

"What do you mean, a 'fox'?"

Andy's lying on the floor, hands behind his head, then he gets up and paces around the room, restless. "You don't know what a fox is? Paulsen, you are so out of it. That's what my cousin Ted calls a good-looking girl."

I laugh. "She's seventy-four years old."

"So . . . are they like lezzies or something?"

"Lezzies?" I know what Andy's talking about. I'm just trying to buy some time to figure out what I'm going to say.

"You know, like . . . girlfriends."

"Yup."

Maybe I shouldn't have said it, because it was Aunt Magda and Miss Nesbit's business. And the last thing I would want would be Andy telling his mother, who would not only blab it to somebody else but would also try to save them, and before you know it the whole town would be talking about poor dead Vandy Paulsen's aunt from Mankato who was, well, you know. *A little strange.*

But it's a test. I want to see what Andy says, how he responds. If he says "gross," well, I'll know. I'll know what I might be up against.

"Well, I suppose that's cool," Andy says.

"Cool? As in okay?"

"Sure, why not? There's lots of gay people in Minneapolis. I mean, it's not like I knew any when we lived there, but they're there."

"I know. I've read about it in the paper." *And I want to be one someday.*

"It must be weird for your aunt and her friend to live out here in the middle of nowhere Minnesota, with no other lezzies around."

"Maybe. But they've always seemed to like it in Mankato. What about two guys?"

Andy frowns. "Two guys?"

"To be a couple, I mean."

"Hm. I'd have to think about that one." Andy tries to balance his pencil, sharpened end down, on the tip of his finger, then on the tip of his nose. It leaves a smudge that I want to reach out and wipe away, but I don't. "I guess you just have to live and let live. That's what my mom always says when my dad cuts down black people."

"So if two guys were a couple, it wouldn't bother you?"

"We'd better get back to work," Andy says. He picks up the book he'd thrown and hands it to me. "I gotta turn things around in Spanish. Otherwise I can forget about ever getting my license."

He didn't say *No, it wouldn't bother me, because I'm madly in love with you and only you.* On the other hand, he didn't say *God, yes, the very thought makes me want to puke.*

I'm willing to take whatever I can get.

We sit on the floor next to each other, our backs against Andy's bed. As usually happens when we try to study together, Andy lasts about five minutes before he's looking for some other distraction: doodling, launching paper airplanes, studying his fingernails (the "boy" way, of course—like you're looking at your fist, the palm side up—and not the "girl" way—holding your hand out in front of you and spreading your fingers. Something else I learned from Andy). He gets up and paces from the window to the door, then back again.

"Have you ever gotten high?"

Andy knows that I haven't. But it's probably the easiest way for him to bring the subject up. "Have you?"

"A few times. With my sister. She had some. Man, it was great. We went out to the barn and did it."

"So where'd she get it?"

"Her boyfriend. He . . . deals it. Don't tell anybody I told you."

"I won't."

"Promise?"

"I promise. Cross my heart and . . ." And then I stop. That's what kids say. *Grow up,* I think. *Be a man.*

"He said he'd sell some to me, but I don't have any money. She let me have some of hers."

"Just because?"

"Well, she can be nice when she wants to be, believe it or not. I think she just asked me because she's afraid to be in the barn by herself at night and she really wanted to get high."

"What was it like?"

Andy slowly closes his eyes until they're little slits. "Man, it's great. I mean, you still know what you're doing and everything, but it's like you're just . . . a little bit off. In a good way, though. You sort of don't care . . . about anything. You can just feel a lot of . . . things."

"What kinds of things?"

Andy opens his eyes, looking a little annoyed at my questions. "Well, like music. It just sounds . . . better." He sways a little bit and hums. "Like you can hear things that you'd miss if you weren't high. It's like . . . *everything's* better. You sort of have to be there. If you've never been high, then you wouldn't really . . ."

"I know. I wouldn't get it." Suddenly I'm angry, but angry with myself, mostly, for not being . . . *with it*. But of course it's mainly Andy I'm angry with, for not including me in the first place. For not believing that I *could* be with it, if he'd just give me half a chance.

I try to go back to Spanish, but I can't concentrate. Andy starts singing "More Than a Feeling," a song from the 1970s that he's become completely and totally obsessed with. It's by Boston—that was the name of the group, not the city, he told me. His uncle, who once saw them in a concert, bought the CD for him at a secondhand record store. Andy loved the picture on the CD cover almost as much as the album itself because from one angle it looked like a guitar on fire, but when you turned it around, it was a spaceship. "That is so cool," he said the first time he showed it to me, flipping the jacket over and over. "Isn't that cool?"

"Sort of like an optical illusion," I said.

"Yeah," Andy said. "It's a delusion, all right."

After that Andy played the album every chance he got, both at his house (so loud it made my head pound, and when I got home I had to take a couple of aspirin) and at mine too (much softer after my father knocked on the door and told us to keep it down, because the floor was vibrating and Anna was trying to nap). Andy, with his short attention span, quickly got tired of most of the songs, but not "More Than a Feeling." I helped him write down the lyrics so he could sing along with it, and after a while he had them memorized. I could hear my father's voice in my head: *You know, if that kid put half as much time into his homework as he did learning that song, he'd be a lot better off.* That was probably true, of course. But it didn't matter to me. I felt like the song belonged to both of us. And when he sang it, he was singing it only for me. I didn't have to share it—or him—with anyone. Like something out of a sappy movie, I know, but I couldn't help it.

Andy's trying to distract me now, playing air guitar and swiveling his hips as he sings, full and confident, even if it's slightly off-key, almost matching the high, throbbing voice of the lead singer. On his fourth time through, he pulls off his T-shirt, twirls it around a few times over his head, and throws it on the floor, like he's doing a strip-tease, though he'd say he's a rocker, not some stripper. That would be too gay. He dances over to his dresser, opens the top drawer, and tosses something to me. It's long and white, like a cigarette, but a lot rounder.

"Do you want to?" he asks.

"Where'd you get this?"

"I just told you. My sister."

"I thought you said you didn't have any money."

Andy sits down next to me, his chest and stomach shiny with his sweat, the sour smell of his underarms starting to fill the room. "Okay, okay, I stole it from her," he says. I watch the thin silver chain that he wears around his neck move up and down. "She'll never miss it."

"Maybe we should study for a while and then try it."

"Paulsen, you're hopeless." He grabs me by the back of my neck and shakes me, but not hard, more playful, his hand warm and sticky on my skin. I want him to leave it there, and then lean over, slowly, and kiss me. I close my eyes and picture it. If I think hard enough about it, maybe I can make it happen.

"So, do you want to get high or not?"

Junauda Petrus is a writer, playwright, screenwriter, and performance artist. With Erin Sharkey, she cofounded Free Black Dirt, an experimental arts production company. Her work centers around wildness, Afro-futurism, ancestral healing, sweetness. Her first novel, *The Stars and the Blackness Between Them,* debuts in 2019 from Dutton Children's Books.

Obituary for Suki, an Old Black Lesbian Who Was Loved

My baby, Suki, was fine. She was dark and smooth and made me understand God through lovemaking and laughs. She listened to Al Green records obsessively sometimes for mental health (she felt he understood her), and Sarah Vaughan for spiritual rituals.

She rolled spliffs of sweet tobacco, marijuana, and blue lotus, and after dinner she liked to smoke on the porch in her rocking chair. A "perfectly good chair" she found in the alley. I painted it turquoise so she could rock and smoke and relax. She was my baby. An avid gardener, she grew tomatoes that were green and striped, purple and fuzzy, or yellow with red centers. She grew corn, greens, basil, oregano, onions, lavender, sweet potatoes. She grew okra. She was the kind of woman who had patience for things that took time and nurturing. She drank whiskey if it was raining or a Monday.

She was a painter who painted me, mostly, and dahlias. The best slow-dance partner. She paid the bills by working as a plumber or a baker on the graveyard shift or a law clerk. This is when paintings didn't sell. When we were planning a trip she did odd jobs on the weekends. She had another woman once, but I think that was it.

We were nineteen when she walked into the library wearing a second-hand, hunter green, three-piece suit and tigereye cuff links inherited from her favorite grandfather. I was researching backpacking through Europe, just in case I didn't pass chemistry that semester.

She was carrying a sketch pad and told me she wanted to sketch me for her portfolio. In other words, she wanted to make love that night and do my astrological chart while listening to Ornette Coleman. And smoke my reefer. She brought me to the rooftop of her tenement, and we saw the moon was full and laid in its blue light, naked, and made seven wishes apiece.

Mine: Lose my virginity, lose ten pounds (without losing my butt), quit smoking cigarettes, move out of my mom's house, meet Tina Turner, learn how to fight, pass chemistry

Hers: Dance on *Soul Train*, find who stole my bike (and whoop they ass), perfect my peach cobbler, get over my fear of flying, learn how to play guitar like an ol' blues man, try LSD (once), travel the world with this woman I am laying naked with in the moonlight

She built things out of old and forgotten shit. She thought everything could be reborn. She collected a lot of crap. She made some of it reusable again. Some of it was stacked neatly in her workroom, awaiting its second coming. She died in my arms, not by herself, even though she was taking this journey alone. Her first trip without me. She is survived by me.

Trina Porte is half New Yorker, half Minnesotan. New York taught her to dissent in the face of oppression; Minnesota, calmness in the face of abuse. Anthologies: *Just Like A Girl, lifeblood, Nickel Empire, Slant of Light.* Favorite venues: Bet Gabriel Center, Bluestockings, public libraries, Vulva Riot. Eternal thanks to her parents' speaking up for equality every day, everywhere.

Elegy Between Middle Age and Death

Say aloud all the names of those who've ever loved me—
even if we haven't spoken in years or they are
long dead themselves or I am dead to them,
lodged in their vault of anger
like forgotten bones bleached white
from so many lost touches no longer adorning
this once precious flesh.

Put my dead body—or what's left after the good parts,
if any remain, have been donated to help
someone keep living as long as
they vow not to hurt anyone (as if that
were possible for a human being
or any breathing creature not to do).

Put what is left of me into the earth or the ocean—
I always loved the ocean because it is
continually raging, massively beautiful,
stronger than all mankind, and touches everywhere.
Or put me into the compost heap if that is where
my beloved ex-wife will lay down her remains
with the last of her garden's sustenance and
her silent love and her raucous laughter, and there
we will remain remains ever after.

There, let the rain raft us to the roots of a flower or
the body of a worm digesting chocolate-rich dirt
who becomes lunch in the belly of a reptile
or amphibian because I dearly loved the snakes,
the turtles, miniscule red efts, and especially the frogs—
their amazing internal antifreezing winter hibernations
and unending shrill singing that defined each spring's arrival.
Yes, put me there in eternal lovely muddy singing spring.

Not their real names

The dollar says "e pluribus unum; out of many, one"
and that's the problem—
we ain't one, y'all. And I'm not co-opting black english:
I learned "y'all" from a white girl in my fifth-grade class.
She was from georgia and proud of it.
I remember her long wavy brown hair
and how included I felt when she said that,
like she meant: Everyone.

Everyone lucky enough to land at ellis island
because they got to choose freedom.
Everyone unluckily brought here in chains,
forging our prosperity with their blood.
Everyone unluckily trusting europeans' deadly gifts
of fetid blankets, and bottled spirits that kill more slowly—
your soul dying generations ahead of your body.
Today's ruination: mail-order brides
sexually enslaved for the price of admission,
committed to hell until death does his part.

We need a new way to be american,
a way to be ourselves.
Named and sacred as who we are born to be,
free of others' ancestral requirements.
I am not of ancient rome, so you can keep your
unums to yourself, thanks.

We are not all one, we are each unique—
"being the only one of its kind;
distinctive, special, unrepeated, rare, uncommon."
I want to know what my real name is,
the one my jewish russian french abenaki
great-great-grandparents would have called me
if they had been allowed to have their own names.

WILLIAM REICHARD

William Reichard is an author, editor, and educator. His sixth poetry collection, *The Night Horse: New and Selected Poems*, was published by Brighthorse Books in 2018.

Midwest Landscape: The First Man

He'd been the mayor for thirty years, town veterinarian, mentor of fatherless boys. He took them along on house calls to isolated farms to treat sick cattle, injured dogs. Or drove them to town to buy their first suits for prom or graduation. After the sheriff found him dead, the top of his head opened up to the sky, shotgun still in his hands, each secret he thought he'd kept began to speak. How many had there been since he'd moved to town? Whose sons were so ashamed of what he'd done to them, they could never speak it, had buried it so deep it finally spilled out in closed fists, stolen prescriptions? Scandal in a small town where most are related by marriage or blood can tear the peace apart, but a good town knows how to silence its own. The residents willed themselves to forget. Still, he'd named each street in the new subdivision after his children. Once the truth was revealed, nobody knew what to do. In the end, the street names remained, but no one mentioned that man again.

Perfect

Nothing is perfect, except, perhaps, the ice,
the way it quietly cracks as the waiter
refills my water glass, and the sun, filtering
down through the newly emerging locust leaves,
refracts in the cold fissures, and turns
a simple glass into a vessel full of light.

None of us has a right to expect perfection.
It's rarely there, and to expect it is to sacrifice
the honest joy we feel when it is achieved.
My eyes, for instance, are not flawless,
nor his chin, nor my hair. Our shirts are, generally,
wrinkled, our clothes, frumpy, and the food
we eat is only routine, despite the pristine reputation
of the restaurant upon whose patio we now sit,
despite the outrageous cost of everything
on the menu, despite our unspoken hope
that the food will be sublime.

This isn't April in Paris. It's May in St. Paul.
The beautiful tulips that border the walls
around the patio seem to strive for transcendence,
but cannot achieve it. The scent of the newly
thawed earth does not give off a perfumed bouquet,
but it's pungently familiar, and comforting.
What's perfect is the fact that the sun has
traveled back to us again, and it dazzles me
as it fills my glass, and I can see,
for a moment, all that's possible.

President Fabulous

I don't think this new president is mine.
Maybe the last one was, but now he's out
on the links, puttering away what's left of
his life. I don't know if there has ever
been a president for me and my kind.
Who is the president of all us little sissies?
Who is president of all of us tomboys,
tough women, weak men? For all of us strung
so beautifully along the sexual continuum,
every one of us, gendered, nongendered,
quasi-gendered, multigendered, omni-all-
and-everything-in-between-gendered?
Who is the president of the queers?
Who is the leader of our free queer world?
I know this new president is not.
I know he's not the president of anything
other than the art of the (bad) deal, art of the steal,
art of the oligarchy of privileged white men
with no imagination and too much cash.
He's not my president if he can't shake his hips,
won't put his lips on any part of another man,
won't raise his legs above his head in that
last, sweet salute. I want a president of the United States
of the Diaphanous, the United States of the Dangerous,
the United States of the Dull, the Fascinating, the Genius,
and the Dumbfounded. A president of the boys, the bois,
the grrrrls, the women, the ladies, the great, the small,
a president for all of us who know,
in the current administration, we have no voice.

The Monster Addresses His Maker
on the Night of His Nuptials

You have fled so far from me that you've run
out of land. You've tried to cross over the top
of the world with your bride. You have failed.
The moment you gave life to me, you became
my beloved. I'm the product of your rib,
Adam born from Adam. You might know
her body, might possess it momentarily,
but you created me, birthed me from the refuse
of the dead. My arms were always meant to
embrace you. In her cabin, she lies cold
as snow, too fragile to survive this rough world.
But my hide is thicker, my body equal only
to yours. See the glacier field, how it stretches
on for miles, disappears into the mouth of the sky?
I've made a wedding chamber there for the two of us.
When they drove me from the village I learned
to live among the trees. Now I crave stillness.
When your legs grow too tired to walk, I'll carry you.
There in the ice, we'll find our perfect balance,
and make our marriage bed our grave.

KATIE ROBINSON

Through poetry, performance, social media fasts, and Epsom salt baths, katie robinson seeks to remember and conjure her liberation. In her work, she draws upon black feminist wisdom to translate her vast reserves of feelings into knowable suggestions of how to practice love.

The Biggest Fish I Follow Follow Ghosts

teeth, all-purpose little early mammal molars

      —Gary Snyder, from "Toward Climax"

last spring,
a young humpback whale
hit our boat in breaching.
before moving along, it turned to examine us.
i looked into the glass case
of its eye and saw family
as it dissolved back into the gray-blue water.

i've known for a while
    that the precursor to a whale
    was a land creature
    a tiny thing
    with deer feet
    that didn't eat fish.

i know that ghosts are responsible for the knowing in me
relics open my mouth in thirst
my neuro-pathways were woven by billions of
lives in crisis.

ghosts and the crisis lives of others
held my bones in fire to bend just before I was born,
ghosts and the crisis lives of others keep me just wet enough under
    my skin to survive,

i am a collection of centuries of molecular agreements screaming
    about the best way to live,
it could be no other way.

i've never known the crisis of going back into water.
    i've never known the flood-carved lungs
    of generations of new ghosts
    or the work of whittling fins to legs and hooves and back again,
    though i imagine the ghosts that agree to be whales do.

i imagine the millions of years of crisis it took the tiny thing with
    deer feet to swim
i imagine how foreign the water
i imagine the fear, the doubt
i imagine how violent their hunger
their disgust at the first taste of sea
i imagine the indigestion
the vomit
the nightmares
the frustration
imagine the denial
the failure
and the death.

i imagine their disbelief
peering out at the sloshing edge of their home
that such a blue and weightless mass would agree to be their skin.

DUA SALEH

Dua Saleh is a multidisciplinary performing artist based in Minneapolis. Dua has previously been granted funding through VERVE, Wellstone Action, 20% Theatre, Phillips Foundation, US Human Rights Network, and more. Dua's art is in conversation with people at the margins of reality, transcending traditional classifications of identity.

Displaced Ancestry

In school they read books printed on flammable paper.
At any moment a misplaced ember could fall at my fingertips, a spark
    could erupt, and each glimpse at history would vanish into dust.
It startled me when I realized it.
Knowledge became as fleeting as misplaced identity.
Identity as temporary as conquest.
Conquest, nothing more than charred skin.
I no longer fear being burned to the ground, because I've been
    unwritten in history.
In these books, no one cares to learn my name.
The only remnants of my truth cloud the sky in congested fogs as
    the pages singe my irises.
In school they read books printed on white paper.
I look at the gaps between each word, in search of my name.
        The one they lost in the war.
My name.
Wrapped in silence.
My name.
Wrapped in empty homes.
My name.
Wrapped in quiet anger that engulfs my dulled tongue.
Your name swells my throat,
bleeds my voice out
        until it drips on white paper.
In school they read books printed on my body.
Their eyes gouge out of their loose sockets.

Their lips quivering, salivating for the permanence of my undying
    breath.
They want to know how I survived the fire.
How my voice has outgrown a mere footnote.
How my shrine lays strewn with remnants of an identity, whole.
My coffin more than a splinter in the ground.
My bones more than a marrow-filled outline.
My ashes more than scattered thought.
In school we read books that have no start or finish.
Each page escapes my name.

Oh Doctor, Who Art in Heaven

Forgive me, doctor, for I have sinned.

When I asked you to listen last, you offered me the blistered eardrum of a forgotten prophet

Called yourself God and

Told me to lower my voice.

Because you might not hear your truth over the volume of my voice.

You said I talk too loud for you to listen.

And maybe you're right.

Maybe I should take all this black and stuff it back down my throat.

Make it easier for you to hear.

Or stomach.

But even if I did, you would never hear all of it. Not at once.

I can. I do.

I hear the voices of children echo off the hallowed chamber of a poisoned oak tree.

Its history gutted out. Its body now a casket for my life.

You said you like to keep the bodies contained.

Makes it easier to muffle the screaming.

You thanked me for bearing such a strange fruit.

One that always dangles on a branch too high for me to reach.

Eventually you jumped and snapped the branch in half. Swallowed me whole.

Fashioned a chair out of my body after skinning me alive.

Drying my skin to a comfortable stretch. Complimenting my hide.

You later thanked me for giving you a front-row seat to my trauma.

In every confession after that moment my voice became a shadow of my truth.

My body grew into a solemn melted core of doubt.

My truth stripped bare from my chest.

Maybe I should stop performing,

Maybe if I stop talking the poison will ripen my memories.
Leave them thick enough for you to choke on.
Keep the doctors away for a moment.
Keep an audience away for a lifetime.
Forgive me, doctor.
Eventually you can find me,
A rotten orchard of dew.
A burden-tinted harvest.
A shallow gathering of generational trauma.
Me alone.
Always.
I'll be nourishing these frozen roots for centuries to come.

Our Doctor, Who art in heaven, hallowed be Thy name; Thy kingdom come; Thy will be done on earth as it is in heaven. Give this Black Dyke a daily piece of bread; and forgive him for trespasses as he forgives those who trespass his body; and lead him not into temptation. Deliver him from evil. And wash away the poison.

Forgive me, doctor, for I always sin.
I've lowered my voice and gaze.
Maybe you can hear me someday.

LUCAS SCHEELK

Lucas Scheelk is a white, autistic, trans, queer-identified poet originally from the Twin Cities, now living in Washington. Their work has been featured in *Barking Sycamores, Assaracus,* and *QDA: A Queer Disability Anthology,* among others. They were one of the twenty-four poets included in the 2017 Saint Paul Almanac IMPRESSIONS Project.

Containers

I encountered a prescription of testosterone in a container labeled SOMEDAY, and for a moment, I mistook it for someone else's.

The container was old. The handwriting was mine. The word SOMEDAY was crossed out and worn down.

The inside of the container reeked of alcohol. Made in 2010 and just as potent.

Within it held the knife I almost used to cut off my breasts. That would have been my last Thanksgiving, if I was left alone.

I was surprised that the clothes hanger from my 22nd Fall wasn't there. I count myself lucky that the biggest reminder of that night was years of tax refunds used to pay off the ambulance I couldn't afford.

The other old containers labeled SOMEDAY are in another box, with the word SOMEDAY crossed out and worn down on each.

I've found new containers labeled SOMEDAY, hidden here and there like Easter eggs.

Sooner than I expected.

Sooner than I wanted.

Each time, I initially mistook the container for someone else's.

Can you blame me for not recognizing them immediately without alcohol this time?

The handwriting was mine. Freshly written. Nothing crossed out.

Divided between the routine of save-that-task-for-a-later-date evasion, and confronting indecision, the concept of genderfluidity, of being nonbinary, and what that means to me, if it means anything to me, overwhelms.

I'd settle for not getting misgendered as is.

I don't want my death to be the occasion to disclose the newest evolution of my self-love.

Choking on the Ashes of Decomposing Depressive Episodes

It is nonstop it is daily it is reaching my hands out to the phoenix for a single tear as I'm choking on the ashes of decomposing depressive episodes

It is nonstop it is daily it is sometimes phoenix tears rain down my arms as a coat of protection but blessings do not erase history

Homelessness doesn't disappear when exalted to Emerging Artist status

Mental illness doesn't create kindness when empathy loses to paranoia

Maladaptive coping doesn't vanish if suddenly employed after long absence

It is nonstop it is daily it is reaching my hands out to the phoenix for a single tear as I'm choking on the ashes of decomposing depressive episodes

It is nonstop it is daily it is sometimes phoenix tears rain down my arms as a coat of protection but blessings do not erase history

Crumbling foundations doesn't fix itself on a Good Day

Crumbling foundations doesn't fix itself with romantic getaways

Crumbling foundations doesn't fix itself with international homestays

It is nonstop it is daily it is reaching my hands out to the phoenix for a single tear as I'm choking on the ashes of decomposing depressive episodes

It is nonstop it is daily it is sometimes phoenix tears rain down my arms as a coat of protection but blessings do not erase history

Rising I work to not sink down those around me it is nonstop it is daily

Rising I work to be strong enough to wash the ashes off me it is nonstop it is daily

Reaching my hands out to the phoenix for a single tear sometimes phoenix tears rain down my arms but blessings do not erase history

Blessings do not erase history but please bless me with the strength to stop choking

ERIN SHARKEY

Erin Sharkey is a writer, producer, educator, and graphic designer based in Minneapolis. She is the cofounder, with Junauda Petrus, of an experimental arts production company called Free Black Dirt (freeblackdirt.com). Her newest project has her studying the soil and the stars and the sorcery of urban farmers.

Grapefruit

Grandma cut the bright orb in half, with the heel of her hand packed the face of each side with brown sugar, then opened the bottom drawer of the oven and broiled the halves until the brown sugar turned liquid.

There were special spoons, more pointed than a soupspoon and narrow like a teaspoon. Their heads covered with tiny teeth, meant to dig in each pocket for flesh. The bites had no hint of bitterness sometimes associated with the pink juice, just bright and sour and sweet.

She found the membrane between each carpel and slipped the spoon along the rind, deep into the pulp, until it was only juice. I did the same, following her lead. Grandma taught us to eat as Danes did. She kept carrots and celery standing in cold water in the fridge, waiting for us. Always open-faced sandwiches on dark rye toast, a thin layer of butter and then some sort of schmear or salad like chicken or egg or ham or tuna, piled on top. Always kringle, raspberry or pecan, the pastry that put the Danes on the map, waiting in the deep freezer for company to come over. And grapefruit on special mornings, like before heading out to cross-country ski on the edge of the property.

Years later, I tried to share this part of my memory with a woman I wanted to know me. We traveled down the curving mountain road to town in a borrowed car. In the market, we held grapefruit in our hands, smelled their buttons for sweetness, bounced our wrists to feel the weight of them, and settled on two sun-colored globes.

Back up the mountain, in our little kitchen, we moved around each other. One of us tall, reaching up to the highest shelf, the other low, near the ground inspecting the broiler drawer. A dance. I fumbled with the latch, couldn't remember if the door was meant to be open or closed. The oven different from my grandmother's. I was making it up from my memories of the way she moved a path from task to task. I was then unsure of the timing, how long to leave them, if looking would wreck the magic.

Her hand was on my lower back. *Why do you think they're called grapefruit?* Watching the closed drawer, willing them to not cook too long. Her hand traveled up my back. A tenderness, a reassurance. *Because they cluster close on the tree.*

When we judged they were ready, when the brown glossed the top, we carried them onto the porch, passed roommates lounging in the living room in various positions with books and knitting and the business of rolling a joint, and onto the deck and into the sun.

We climbed up and laid on our bellies on the picnic table, our shoulders close together, and struggled with smooth-edged spoons. We made a mess of the sweetness, could not keep the skins in the radial pattern with our clumsy instruments. Not frustrated but excited for the excuse, she lifted the bowl of the peel to her lips and drank the nectar; let the sticky juice coat her fingers.

When the skins of the fruit were picked clean, we flipped on to our backs and watched the sky.

Grandma taught me how to do that, as well. To let the snow hold your fatigued body, to slow your breathing, to celebrate the labor, even when it wasn't smooth, when your clumsy skis found the glide for only a few strides at a time. To be silent together, wondering if the other sees the hawk far off on a high branch, or the way the wispy white clouds move slowly across the sky.

Rodented Away

After the last time we made love . . . had sex . . . fell into it . . . didn't stop . . . did that thing we wont talk about . . . crossed the line . . . gave in to the pull . . . did what we both desperately wanted . . . needed . . . were compelled to do . . . a mouse ran the edge of the baseboard, the closet, the corner, under window . . . paused a moment . . . braved the doorway. The small hole to the place I will never know. The hoard of gathered things. The world a whole different scale, fibers, grains, a family huddled together for warmth.

Her back. The shiny wap of cars driving over wet leaves given up to the ground . . . her back, its soft armor. Breathless and out of harm's way.

When you're in high school you don't meet, walk up to your peer, extend your hand, confirm how you know one another, exchange pleasantries. It's more like "What did Colletti say was due tomorrow?" or "Can you pass the bowl of slip?"

And then you silently let the other girl watch as you gently coax the earth spinning on the wheel with your wet hands and their micro muscles to rise, to push with your thumbs, make a well, to birth a bowl . . . to take a sponge and rain water on the vessel and lower that cloud and smooth its edges. Imagine all that fingers can make. And she will remember you as the girl who shaped the earth . . .

And then she lets you watch her make spells with the glaze, to evoke the hidden colors, with faith that the heat will make it beautiful. You will always remember her secret mixture.

We have a hoard.

Rodented away in a small dark place.

The edges of her, their pull, the willing me back in, even as her face turned toward the wall, looked through it, made a hole there, willed herself to a place she could squirrel away her desire . . . a free place where she could desire, desire she could trust. Let a shiny surface inside her replicate my skin, my glint of teeth, my rough hair, dance on her, with her dancing.

Christine Stark is an award-winning author and visual artist of white, Anishinaabe, and Cherokee heritage. Her writing has appeared in numerous publications. Her first novel, *Nickels: A Tale of Dissociation,* was a Lambda Literary finalist. Her poem "Momma's Song" was recorded by Fred Ho and the Afro Asian Music Ensemble as a manga CD. For more information: www.christinestark.com.

The Bovine Babes

Alix was a six-foot-two, gangly forty-five-or-so-year-old goalie who lived in the suburbs, called her partner "wife," had children, and was very good at punching the ball over the top of the net. A detective with the Madison police department, she always seemed a bit above the rest of us on the Bovine Babes, Wisconsin's only all-lesbian soccer team (except for that one straight girl). Alix never hung out with the team. She did not act superior, but she did, after all, live in the burbs and have a wife—a term no one used in the Madison lesbian scene in the early 1990s. (At that time, most of us were transitioning from using *girlfriend* to the more palatable *partner*. I preferred *girlfriend*, although I acknowledged its drawbacks.) Perhaps Alix seemed especially untouchable to me because I may have, at times, unconsciously interacted with her from the space of reverence a younger (and shorter) version of me desperate to know I was not the "only one" would have held for an older (and exceptionally tall) role model who had a grown-up lesbian life.

God knows I knew something was up since I was three, living in a rented house on a farm in Sleepy Eye, Minnesota, next to and across the highway from two Catholic families that lived in massive farmhouses. I viewed the approximately thirty children from the two families with a bit of fear and wariness. My parents and I lived in a tiny, one-story house probably built for the farmhands. They lived in majestic farmhouses with gleaming oak woodwork and ceiling beams, winding staircases, and Hail Mary fonts mounted on the frames outside the children's bedroom doors. Mother Mary's toes, curled over the edge of the bowl she stood on, were about even with the top of my head. The children dipped their fingers into the bowls and crossed themselves. I don't recall knowing it was "holy water," even though I was dragged to St. Mary's Catholic Church every Sunday morning. (My parents taught elementary school there.) That may have been when my habit of "not listening" to things I did not like began, which could be why I didn't know what was in the bowl. Mostly, that blue lady and her toes made me nervous and unsure about the others around me. It was the beginning of knowing I didn't belong.

I was three when I knew I was different *different* from the other kids. One day my babysitter, Irene, held out two dolls, one for me and one for her four-year-old daughter. *Which one do you want*, she said to me, holding the cloth dolls in front of my face. *Pick one*. I did not want a doll. *No*, I said over and over. *Yes*, she said over and over. Once it became apparent she was going to make me take one, and I would have to, yet again, yield to an adult, I pointed at the boy doll. If I had to have a horrible doll, the one in the blue square shorts was less worse than the one in the dress, an item I never wore if I could help it. *Okay*, Irene said, gleefully. Glumly, I took the doll and turned away, anxiety for being "not right" trailing alongside me. I don't remember what I did with the doll, but I know I never played with it. I had no interest in dolls—ever. I liked petting the cows, pigs, cats, and dogs on the farm and studying the rows of plants poking their little arms up through the black dirt alongside the rented house.

Thinking more about Alix, it's also possible I felt "reverence" for her because I'm a bit afraid of cops. Regardless, Alix's lanky physique, bumble-bee goalie shirt, and oversized white goalie gloves anchored our team as we trained for the 1994 Gay Games IV in New York City. Truth was, I didn't think Alix was all that good, but I never said anything. I didn't even want to think it. I had finally found a place I belonged *belonged*, and I did not want to be different from my teammates. I had to be careful about not being too competitive. After all, I was All-State in high school and played Big Ten Badgers' soccer, which in the lesbian soccer world was like being a B-list celebrity.

I liked Alix well enough, but I was skeptical that we could win the Gay Games with her. (And I wanted to win!) She didn't have the quickest reflexes. She was nothing like the goalie on my high school team when I was a junior and we won state—Patty was an explosive athlete who could dunk a Nerf ball. Although, perhaps they were not all that unlike each other. Patty and Alix were both new to the teams—recruited to goaltending because my high school and Gay Games teams needed goalies. And, as a sixteen-year-old lesbian always living below the surface of the rest of the (straight) boys and girls, I had a pretty good idea what Patty and the goalie coach, only a few years older than Patty, were doing all those hours alone together in the windowless room with the royal blue wrestling mats strewn about. It was 1984, and I did not know of anyone who was "out." I was nervous about how obvious they were being. I looked away a lot, afraid for them and afraid for me. Starting in elementary school, I interacted with people knowing they knew. And I knew they knew I knew. So I'd been finely tuned by the time I was in high school to watch my step. *You can go this far, but not that far* controlled my thoughts and actions. *Don't touch other girls. (Unless you're plowing into them on the field or court.) Be careful where your eyes land in the locker room. Control your breathing while lying next to the girl you want to kiss at the sleepover. Don't show yourself.*

I don't recall how I found the Bovine Babes. Maybe they found me. Probably we met in the neighborhood, because, except for the two radicals in the 'burbs, all the lesbians in Madison in the 1990s lived near or in Dyke Heights. (I always wondered if straight people who resided in Dyke Heights knew where they were living.) Shortly before joining the team, I'd ditched my family because my mother told me my aunts and uncles would not let my recently out lesbian aunt attend family functions as she might sexually abuse my girl cousins. The prevailing thought in my family at that time was that lesbians are sexual predators, so when my aunt finally came out (everyone knew about her, too), not only was she no longer welcome in the family, she was considered a threat to the family—a rapist. Apparently, this did not apply to my great-uncle Jerry, a flaming gay man who lisped and sashayed his way through numerous 1960s and '70s church-basement potlucks (Oh, those lemon bars!) as a brother in the Catholic Church. Everyone knew he was gay, yet when my father once said Jerry was gay, Jerry's brother threatened to kill my father. Around 8:00 one night, the winter I also happened to be eight, after a frenetic phone call between my mother and an aunt, I received instructions to not answer the door for or let my other great-uncle in our house, now a split-level in the 'burbs. I'm not sure if my mother told me he was going to shoot my father or if it was more of a generic "He says he's going to kill your father," but I spent quite a few months with my nerves on high whenever I walked in front of the living room windows—overcome by vivid mental images of me hitting the deck to avoid the spray of bullets as my gangster great-uncle drove by in his station wagon.

Alix anchored our team because that's what goalies do in soccer, but the Bovine Babes was not just any soccer team; we were a lesbian soccer team, and lesbian teams can get dicey at times. Once, while playing basketball in Madison, there was a shout and a slam and then the ball shot straight up off the court, nearly reaching the ceiling. Everyone on both teams froze as if we were all mysteriously transported to a 1970s backyard game of "statue." The shouter/ball bouncer glared at one of my teammates. No one moved. It was like we all knew, without having any direct knowledge of what was happening, that this was about what we'd all suppressed. Among us collectively existed hundreds of years of denying and hiding our sexual desire, and then it erupted in the shape of that basketball spinning up among the rafters. Finally, some brave soul retrieved the ball that had rolled to a corner of the gym, the stare-down ended, and we resumed play. Later Monica, who was most likely responsible for inviting me to play on the Babes, told me one of them had slept with the other's girlfriend. *Ahh,* I said. But of course I knew.

Finding the Babes and all the other glorious lesbians on Madison's east side saved me from the homophobia of not only my childhood but also the university's athletic department. When my teammate's parents discovered there were lesbians in the athletic department they demanded she leave for a Catholic university. We lesbians were so—what? horrific? powerful? predatory? sinful? catching?—that our mere presence in an office meant their daughter needed to leave the entire university and even the state. Another time, at a team drinking party (UW women's soccer would make national news a decade later for underage drinking and brawling at the Stadium Bar—the same place we drank) my straight teammates made fun of the other lesbian on the team. I don't recall even talking with the other lesbian during the two years we were both on the team. They'd found a letter from her girlfriend and read it out loud. *She says she loves her legs and can't wait for her to return so she can run her hands over them.* I was guzzling from a beer bong at the time. As one of them poured more beer from a pitcher into the funnel held above my head, I kept right on drinking, sucking down beer as fast as it cascaded through the rubber tubing, while they laughed at our teammate, her girlfriend, me.

When I joined the Bovine Babes we were the Dairy Queens, but not for long. Dairy Queen—that red-roofed corporation where I'd been slurping cherry Mister Mistys since I was six—caught wind of our name (how, I have always wondered) and threatened to sue our straggly collection of lesbian soccer butts. We were not a powerful soccer club. We were not connected with a school. But we were "powerful" enough that simply by attaching *Dairy Queens* to *lesbian* meant we had a potential lawsuit. I remember thinking, *Wow! Straight people sure don't like us!* (While it's possible that Dairy Queen would have sued any local amateur team, we understood it to be a perpetuation of straight people's hysterical fear of lesbians.) An emergency team meeting was called. We had to register soon with the Gay Games committee and needed a new name. We packed into my girlfriend-at-the-time Jen's bungalow in Dyke Heights. After much conversation, we settled on the Bovine Babes, which I thought a better fit anyway. (While both names referenced Wisconsin as the Dairy State, *Queen* does, after all, technically refer to gay men.)

Once we agreed on the Bovine Babes, we had a lot of work to do, not only on the field but off it. We needed a strong center midfielder, a fund-raiser, uniforms, and a place to stay, as a hotel would have been too expensive. (I wished for a goalie like Patty, but I kept that to myself.) Monica (right midfielder) and I (center forward) took charge of the fund-raiser. Along with her ex-girlfriend, who was a musician (and thankfully not a soccer player or dating anyone on the team), we organized three bands to play at the Barrymore Theatre in Dyke Heights. Tina and the B-Sides from Milwaukee, a Madison-based band whose name I do not recall, and Minneapolis's own Babes in

Toyland agreed to play, as long as we paid expenses. We all knew Tina was a lesbian, but her straight audience did not. Those were the days lesbians went to see k.d. lang, Melissa Etheridge, and others knowing they were dykes and watching all the straight people dancing along with their favorite (closeted) lesbians. Our bemusement and annoyance at the straight folks acting as if one of *ours* was one of *theirs* was one way we resisted being invisible, as if we did not exist.

The fund-raiser was a success, covering transportation and food for eighteen players to the Big Apple—but not a hotel. Tina invited us onstage with the band. *They're the Bovine Babes and they're going to the Gay Games!* she shouted. Surprised, as being called up was not part of the plan, our team climbed the steps to the stage. The largely college-age heterosexual audience stood slack-jawed as eighteen dykes danced with their beloved band, led by a not-out-to-the-crowd lesbian. (Tina came out a few years later.) I boogied in my belted, low-slung, faded Levi's and cowboy boots, trying to maintain the proud lesbian self I'd grown into like those little plants on the Sleepy Eye farm. Yet, the audience's reaction withered me, bringing back the million and a half times I'd felt less than for being a dyke. As we stepped offstage to scattered claps, I brushed off the stares. After all, with the Bovine Babes, I belonged *belonged*.

Oh, by the way, the Bovine Babes took silver. Alix was rock-solid. I was the leading scorer and enjoyed being admired by throngs of lesbians as I sprinted down the sidelines. Or so I imagined. Too tired to deal with the long train rides that would have enabled us to enjoy the sights of New York City and all those queer bodies, we crashed at the center fullback's aunt's house in Long Island between games. Eighteen Bovine Babes iced various body parts in the aunt's vast living room, gearing up for the next game while watching the white Bronco flee down the freeway in L.A.—again and again. And, much to my chagrin, Monica began dating the left midfielder.

Vanessa Taylor is a writer and organizer living in Minneapolis. They believe in using a multidisciplinary approach to make sense of the world. Their work focuses on exploring Black womanhood and Muslim identity.

salat al kusoof

I cultivated it in a fantasy
that brief template of totality
I crawled to half-moon shadows and
sacrificed a mockery of my skin.

You've been captivated by violence,
children who nurse from blood.
Look at tragedy—how she bears herself;
a royalty you envy, drawing her cloak
close to hide arms.

In that brief window
where you stood like sketches
lined to test your authority against time
my spine folded under its own pressure.

"Isn't it beautiful," you marvel,
"how tragedy pulls a curtain across the sky";
and I? press my forehead
to unforgiving ground.

shattering my sister's confidence

what do the people of the book say of me

you're a whore / slave / you had no choice.
the closest to grace they offer / bitter trade for defamation / settling
    like a sour grape on the grooves of a tongue / worn down by
    desert prayers

/........../

never loved in life / what do you expect?
you were a slave / you had no choice
but you're still a whore.

and the others

understand, sister / you can believe your legacy is defined by water /
it was your son's heel / you were spoken to / promise springs of
abundance / but there is no current strong enough to undo chains /
understand, sister / the earth parted / some say for you / but nobody
wrote you into the script / there is nothing great that comes from us

```
                    pa
            my        th
        run             but
      they                they
    but                     run
        m y p a t h

                    pa
            my        th
        run             but
      they                they
    but                     run
        m y p a t h
```

    buttheyrunmypathbuttheyrunmypathbuttheyrunmypath
they run your path / and still / say
nothing

Bradford Tice is the author of *Rare Earth*, which was named the winner of New Rivers Press's 2011 Many Voices Project, and *What the Night Numbered*, winner of the 2014 Trio Award.

The Dom Poem

—after Pat Califia

You are who I say you are: boy or man, rapture's dregs
lifting from your face. Whatever costume it pleases

me that you don, that's what you bare to the world.
Sometimes I think there is nothing I could do to hurt you

the way you want to be hurt, the way you want to be shown
the scalloped edges of yourself, to lean into it

the way you know you can, knowing I will not
let go your hand. Boy in denim, boy in leather, in nothing

but a jock and socks, and the scent of you sour
in my throat. Isn't this what you wanted? For me to name

what you are? Boy dropped from heaven, sheltered
in my hands, who needs to be taught how hot the irons

get, my belt a message: I hurt you to remind you
that the body is something else we might lose.

You've done the same for me. I leave off the cage's
lock for the pleasure of seeing you stalk the mirror, flesh

angry at your back. How you stand there assured you've felt
the switch, dom turned on, sub off. You draw deep,

nostrils flaring, as if you've scented inside me a felled
animal. Boy aroused by daddy's drunken nakedness.

If I bare to you the throat's vulnerable pulp,
if you bit hard and ate what words you will, who then

would master the other, the meat of us ground together,
both having submitted to an end? Answer me.

Would you eat ashes, rust, if I demanded it?
Answer me. Please. Could you love a man who bends?

The Sub Poem

—after Pat Califia

Be careful: the lick of rawhide on my back
makes strange calligraphy, but can you thumb it
and know? It's no utterance.

All you doms are so damn wedded to your rituals.
The devotions hosannaed once you notch
tighter the restraints, the spit required

to answer your questions: *Do you like that,*
do you want me to hurt you? Being skilled
with a whip doesn't make you sharp.

Once you realize that you pray to a dark god,
face always in shadow, you can become a worshipper
whose doubt has been sharpened to an edge.

When you're inside me, I feel you breaking down
a part of me that resists you, the rubble
left of a temple that I will use to build a city

where I have slept in every house. The submissive
exists to give shape to your demands, the arc
of my back receiving your weight, your cock the arrow

that feathers me. Tell me, who is more brave?
At a party, when a straight acquaintance, whom I'm sure
you thought golden, his body oiled and anointed,

asks, lips upturned, *Which of you sits bitch?*
You chuckle, tell him, *Don't worry, I always drive.*
Is this what it takes to take another man by the shoulder?

Look him in the eye, see relief visible, the fortress's
defenses impenetrable? Perhaps my fondness
for locks is just an awareness of how little

they actually restrain. Daddy, once
you're stripped enough, you can stand exposure.
Later at the party, you will drink too much,

stumble with a little too much license into
the dark outside. I will drive you home to bed,
and when I climb on top your cock, move

above you like a warning in the stars' movements,
careful what you cry out into that listening.
Careful what you hold out your hands to receive.

Ann Tweedy's first full-length book, *The Body's Alphabet,* was awarded a Bisexual Book Award in poetry and was a Lambda Literary Award finalist and Golden Crown Literary Society Award finalist. She has published two chapbooks and has twice been nominated for a Pushcart Prize. She also serves as an attorney for Indian tribes and is a widely cited legal scholar.

Rental Property

When my mother was evicted from public housing, I was in my forties, living fifteen hundred miles away, but I felt like it was happening to me. Did I have bad boundaries? Or had I never gotten over my childhood fear that she and I would lose the house we lived in because she didn't pay the bills? Maybe both. I was teaching property law when she was evicted for hoarding, and it happened during the time I was teaching landlord-tenant law. Bitterly funny. I thought the eviction violated the Fair Housing Act—she has an obvious disability—but her legal services lawyer wouldn't raise the objection. The lawyer thought it wouldn't be fair to the other side—the town housing authority—which had "bent over backwards," so I tried to get a reasonable accommodation request in as a family member. But I don't know if the judge read it.

And anyway, she was evicted. And the social worker assigned to help her started up on some tough love bullshit, arguing that my mother wasn't cooperating because she wasn't at her apartment when the social worker arrived a few minutes early for an appointment— my mother had stepped out to do laundry—and so she wouldn't support my request for my mother to have more time in the apartment before leaving, which meant the other side wouldn't agree to it. I got the news that the eviction went through right before teaching my property law class, and I tried very hard not to cry standing at the front of the big law-school lecture hall.

Later, the minister who had helped clean out the apartment for my mother got her committed, concerned that she had the body of her dead cat in an empty refrigerator. My mother loves cats. She told me once when I was a child and asked her that she didn't know if she

loved me or the cat more. Which is a clear answer to the question—
she loved the cat more. I don't know why children ask such questions. Now when my own son asks them, do you love me more than
the cats, do you love me more than _____, I know the answer. The
answer is always yes. You only have to hear "I don't know" once to
know to say yes to that sort of question forever after. Yes yes yes.
Without any hesitation, without stopping to think about it.

Storms

During Winter Storm Juno, which deposited twenty-four inches of snow in Boston on January 26 and 27, 2015, I call my mother to see if she has shelter. She tells me, *Never worry about me during bad weather. Homeless people luck out during snowstorms.* Apparently, if you care about the homeless, you should wish for perpetual natural disaster. Let nature take its course. The resources will follow.

The truth is, I call my mother after a concerned friend texts me about her. The friend and I are estranged—we have agreed not to be in touch, but sometimes find ourselves engulfed in a brief flurry of texts and emails, even a few phone calls. So far, I haven't called my mother during the next storm, which is happening now. My friend hasn't texted me this time, but that's not it. And it's not that I am not worried. It's more that there would literally be no end to worry if I started that gerbil wheel in my brain.

The gerbil wheel spun full-time when I visited in December. I came to see my father in a Boston hospital, while my mother wandered the streets and subway cars of the same city he lay in, post-surgery. The nurses and doctors checked in every hour as I sat by his bed and thought about my mother, who had nowhere to go, no regular shelter. Sometimes my friend called, and I argued quietly on my cell phone in the hall.

The first day I was there, my mother herself was released from the hospital, as I learned when she called me back that afternoon. A urinary tract infection. The bed was so comfortable and the food so good, she hadn't wanted to leave. She fell asleep in the hospital pharmacy waiting for her prescription and missed the chance to call shelters to see who might have space. When I was little, she worked as a pharmacist at two different Boston hospitals.

That night she missed the chance to apply for the shelters' one-night lotteries by waiting for me at Au Bon Pain. I told her not to meet me and not to wait if it would interfere with finding a place, but she wanted to see me. It was mid-December. She said she could stay in the train station if it was freezing out. My phone read thirty-three degrees. We debated the significance of an extra degree. Then it got to be past midnight, too late to go to the train station anyway—they lock the doors after 12:00. A hotel or a hostel was way too much money, she told me.

Finally, we took the subway to a hostel at 1:30 in the morning. Her legs gave out several times as we walked to the hostel from the subway. She grabbed onto an iron fence, and I held her hand, carried a tote bag bulging with papers. Dehydration from the urinary tract infection, she postulated. And also: *You should call an ambulance. That would be better than the hostel.* And an ambulance would enable her to go to a hospital near a shelter she liked—Rosie's Place—so she would be right there in the morning and wouldn't miss any deadlines. My head spun. Eventually, we made it to the hostel, and I made the last train back to my Airbnb. I'm still at a loss about the ambulance.

Before I visited, she told me that as an elderly person—seventy-seven—she always had a spot in a shelter and could usually stay for weeks or months at each one. Until that night at Au Bon Pain, I'd never felt guilty about having a place to go. There are over six hundred thousand homeless people in America on any given night. But, even for me, that's hard to take in.

I felt strange standing next to her in my BCBG coat at the Harvard Square Shelter that first night, as she knocked at 11:00 PM to see if there had been any no-shows. Then the next night, at 9:00, I stood outside the same door with her as she called to get into the 9:30 lottery. There were about ten people out there, talking while rocking or shifting from foot to foot to bear the cold. *Will my being with you make it worse because they'll think you have a place to go?* I asked. She thought for a moment, then said, *No, better.* And that evening she won the one-night lottery (which was pure coincidence). I wish I knew where she was now.

Anatomy of a Name

My name, the first, something no one
would make fun of, my mother said,
and plain, not because she was looking for plain
but because we are plain, the people
I come from—New Englanders and Upstate
New Yorkers, plain without meaning to be plain
or thinking about plainness but plain just the same.
That may explain the lack of an "e," the "e"
that other Anne, Anne of Green Gables, was so proud of,
her saving grace so to speak, saving her from utter
plainness, and "Ann" means grace after all.
No doubt snobbery was part of it,
my first and middle names the names of queens
as one lover pointed out.

And my last name, the name of a river, I used to tell the kids
who made fun of me, a Scottish river. My cousin
of the same name laughed at the logic
of telling taunting children they were misreading
my name; it had no cartoonish "t" near the end. Even back then
I thought knowledge might save a person.
Of course I got my name from my father and, when I married,
had to ponder if it was mine enough
to hold onto, but I figured by then I'd co-opted it—
having lived with it and fought for it—
even though, as my grandfather's name,
it emblemed family pain.

My mother looked down on made-up names. A poor person
who contrived to seem rich, she saw made-up names and altered
    spellings
as inescapable. I went along at first but gradually grasped
my plain name and my cartoon name
as undeserved legacy—a kinship with history—

instead of slaveholders' names or names doled out
to Indian families during allotment—each family's easiest first name
recast as a surname. Names of oppressors—or chosen by them—
borne into the future by each new baby
undone at last by names sprung from sound,
an act of freedom
to disown plain people like me.

An Instant

After I came home from visiting you,
I didn't want to dry-clean the pink rayon dress I wore
when we walked to breakfast that last day
through July-hot San Antonio streets.
The armpit sweat was mine—anything of you
on the dress—maybe some fragments of dry skin—
would have been microscopic.

But it carried the memory
of how you sat on my lap, looked hard
into my eyes, for a few moments before
we walked outside. Even the blister I got
on my little toe from wearing the wrong shoes
on that walk was a welcome reminder
for weeks afterward.

It was months before I dry-cleaned the dress
and I haven't worn it since, although I will
and that wearing will effect a small erasure
the way that living erases the past.
And dying seems no better because maybe the past
floats up like a cloud and disperses upon death.

Certainly, there is no earthly museum for the pasts
of dead people, and it's hard to imagine them
trapped in one in the underworld, however much
some of us might wish that upon ourselves
when the time before loss
seems the only harbor.

Now, when I think of you, I try to concentrate
on how you would repeat over and over the short time
we saw each other, as though I didn't understand the risks
I contemplated. I remember how I said *I know I know*

only to pick up the phone on the next call and hear again
how the four days was in effect a weekend,
that I didn't know how I would feel
if we were in a relationship. *I know I know*
If I recited the same facts back to you
it didn't matter.

My comfort with the blankness of the future—my willingness
to jump blindfolded into it—somehow translated into
my being trapped on a walk among stately stucco houses,
the sun washing us, the trees multiplying and transmitting
each soft breeze, my wince at the sharp bark of the fenced Chihuahua
instantly bringing your arm around me.

MORGAN GRAYCE WILLOW

Morgan Grayce Willow's poetry titles include *Dodge & Scramble*, *Between*, *Silk*, and *The Maps are Words*. Her nonfiction has appeared in *Water~Stone Review*, *Imagination & Place: Cartography*, *Riding Shotgun*, and *BoomerLitMag*. In 2016 Morgan exhibited her artist's book *Collage for Mina Loy* at the Minnesota Center for Book Arts.

On My Way to John Berryman I Discover Stephanie Brown

I'm thumbing through *The Body Electric*
searching for John Berryman poems
when the title "Schadenfreude" captures my eye.
Of course I must stop, read. A simple syntax,
like piles of laundry, clean but not yet folded,
stacks separated by color and textile
leaning into dishevelment. Yet the pattern
is clear as Saturday afternoon,
and just that simple. A heap of clauses,
one stacked upon another, tossed
like the white sock toward its mate
that somehow got mixed up with T-shirts,
green, gray, indigo. One doesn't expect
a librarian to toss off such languid,
wry lines—Marianne Moore notwithstanding—
each one stretching far across the page.
Blunt narratives about getting high
and having hippie sisters, shredding clichés
like Yosemite Sam with his machete.

But wait. Yosemite Sam doesn't have a machete.
He has six-shooters. I looked it up. And that's
the kind of thing Stephanie Brown would do,
that direct admission spoken straight to the reader,
as if you sat with her across a red Formica table,
its chrome legs curving down from each corner,

little rubber booties on the bottoms to prevent scuffing
the recently polished Armstrong tile floor,
shining bright, no waxy buildup.
You're drinking Cherry Cokes, smoking Marlboros,
in this second-floor college apartment.
The ashtray fills up, while jelly beans gather
in a green Melmac bowl. You're wearing cutoffs,
frayed fringes dancing the circumference of your thighs,
though Stephanie's in striped pedal pushers,
and a neon pink halter top. It's dawn by now.
The two of you simultaneously notice
the pinkening sky in the rectangle of window
between faded chintz curtains above the kitchen sink,
which is full of dirty plates and silverware.
A Pizza Hut box sits on the pink counter tiles nearby.

That's what it's like reading a Stephanie Brown poem.
Now I wonder whether she scribbled
across a yellow legal pad (like this one)
on her desk in the library, a stack of manila acquisitions folders
ready to provide cover when her secretary taps
at the office door to announce the next interview,
or carries long reams of spooled computer paper,
the balance sheet needing to be proofed
before copies can be made for the board,
which meets tonight. And just before
I flip the pages, move on
to John Berryman's Henry-in-recovery poems,
I imagine Stephanie Brown as heroine
in a Roy Lichtenstein comic book,
her blonde hair, her elegant calligraphy eyebrows
above dark eyes, each of which leaks
one perfect tear. It drips to her skintight
red bodice, bearing angular black letters: SP.
Mild-mannered librarian by day,
Super Poet in the interstices of night.

The Way It Is

Much turning
through the swirl and churn
each day brings.
The story we cobble
out of shells
and repetitions.
Our individual planet.
The way my orbit
differs from yours.
The way the border defines
both outside and in.
The way any circle
that seems cut
is never really broken.

I Raise My Eyes to Fred & Ginger

I'm on the floor
working my left piriformis,
trying to stretch away the sciatica
that's been causing my left big toe,
and the one next, to tingle,
easing myself into pigeon pose,
left knee tucked, right leg
straight out behind.
I lower my torso over the knee,
forehead to the mat, then breathe
into the tightness. Exhale.
Visualize tension flowing away
from the hard-to-reach muscle.
But before I can stop them
today's headlines, worse again
than yesterday, impose themselves.
Inhale. Notice them. Exhale.
Let them go. At the bottom
of the next exhale, I sink
for a moment into stillness
and all my grief for the world.

You can't stay here,
my coach self advises,
or you'll never rise
from the weight of it.
So, breathe.
I raise my pigeon chest,
arch my back, and sink
into the painful left hip.
Then, vertebra by vertebra,
I raise my head. Finally,
my eyes, the lids lifting
to the eastern wall.
And there they are, in the very spot

where they appear every morning,
Fred & Ginger having just completed
a twist, the tail end of a wide, sweeping arc
around the polished floor,
caught in the photo
in that fraction of a second
before Ginger spins back the other way,
her sleek gown still wrapped around
her hips and knees.
Fred's weight is in his left foot,
his right about to step
and take their swirl another direction.

Such simplicity, this moment
in their complex dance.
We never know how many rehearsals
went into this perfect pause,
how much her tendons hurt
in those high-heeled shoes,
the crick in his shoulder
from always making it look so buoyant,
whether she balked at his insistence
that they do yet another take,
the pressure of having to get the whole thing right
because there were no second chances
in the editing suite.

How many millions
have watched this by now,
delighted by the improbability,
relieved that the dance goes on,
even now that they are both long gone?
Fred and Ginger dancing
in their pristine back lot world
while the world outside the studio
clambers out of depression
toward war.

S. YARBERRY

S. Yarberry is an MFA candidate in poetry at Washington University in St. Louis. Their work has appeared in, or is forthcoming in, *Bomb Magazine* (interview), *Nat, Brut, FIVE:2:ONE*'s #thesideshow, *Touchstone Magazine, Broken Yolk,* and miscellaneous zines. They are currently editor of The Revue at *The Spectacle.*

Where do your hands go when we sleep?

I press my nose to the back of your neck and you stir.

I want to ask you something. I love waking you. But there's nothing
   to say.

There are so many lives we will
not live together—

· · ·

In one, we live in New York and the cabs buzz like bees.
Busy Bees Have No Time for Sorrow! I chime, as we walk
in our camel coats to everywhere we could think to go.

In another, we sit in the grass
and you laugh, and the parrots dot
the phone lines like dulled holiday lights.

Perhaps in one version of it,
the TV whistles a familiar tune
and you are only far away.

There's this one: where we look at each other across the room—
the lights: dark green, magenta, and maybe a little music
is on somewhere in the back—and I stand there in awe of what I
   have lost.

· · ·

What if this life could hold us both?

• • •

We sleep with the window cracked.
The sky is beginning to turn.

ARIEL ZITNY

Ariel Zitny is a queer trans Jew from California. He performed in Queer Voices in 2015 and lived in Minneapolis for the next two years. He is published in the literary journals *Wild Ones, Vermillion Literary Project,* and *TQ Review*. He is currently in school to become a rabbi.

Morning Blessing

Blessed are you, eternal God, who has molded my soul
from contradictions. From apparent opposites
you have created me, and from within dichotomies
I can see the plurality of your creation. Blessed
are you, eternal God, who has made me trans.

What Is a Queer in Isolation?

I do not assert
my identity in hand
holding face
kissing
visibility

It's more the asexual
spinster
gaygendered
perpetually single
visibility

What is a queer in isolation?

It wasn't a girl
who taught me
I was different
it was third-grade
kids spitting
on the playground

I hadn't realized
it wasn't universal
simply
"some people prefer
blondes, some people
prefer girls."

?

Coming out without
a partner seemed silly
but I did it anyway
"you're too young

to know"
from adults
from friends
"obviously"

the response reverberates
obviously

?

At a gay bar
with my cousin
two queers cruising
instead seen
as *together*

I don't seem
off until I open
my mouth
and someone else's voice
comes out

What is a queer in isolation?

Alone
every family
holiday the
grandparents think

I'm still waiting

The text of *Queer Voices: Poetry, Prose, and Pride* has been set in Calluna, a slab serif text family designed by Jos Buivenga and is a trademark of exljbris Font Foundry.

Book design by Wendy Holdman